Flying Changes

Flying Changes

BY LYNN HALL

Harcourt Brace Jovanovich, Publishers

San Diego   New York   London

HBJ

Copyright © 1991 by Lynn Hall

Library of Congress Cataloging-in-Publication Data
Hall, Lynn.
Flying changes/by Lynn Hall.
p. cm.
Summary: Seventeen-year-old Denny and her
family face hard times when her father is injured on
the rodeo circuit.
ISBN 0-15-228790-6
(pbk.) ISBN 0-15-228791-4
[1. Horses—Fiction. 2. Country life—
Fiction.] I. Title.
PZ7.H1458Fmc 1991
[Fic]—dc20 90-45516

Printed in the United States of America

A B C D E

Flying Changes

Monday, July 10

1

The sun was still a red haze on the horizon, but already I knew this could be the best day of my life, depending on a few words from Tyler.

I sat on the buckskin filly, looking in a circle around myself and giving her time to calm down. There was the house, square and white and as dusty as everything else around here. A truck jack held up one corner of the kitchen porch. Daddy never did get around to fixing that. Wouldn't now, not ever. The yard needed mowing. Tyler said he'd do that yesterday, but then he went off to town and never did it.

Bedsheets hung out on the line behind the house. Gramma B. used the dryer for everything else, but she always hung the bedsheets outside so they'd smell of fresh air. Hung them out at sunset, brought them in before breakfast. It wasn't as dusty at night as in the daytime.

There, parked in the side yard, was Tyler's pride and joy, a Dodge Ramcharger club-cab pickup, brown and tan, with dual wheels on the rear and a charging bull hood ornament. The matching horse trailer was parked in the machine shed with a tarp over it to keep off the bird doo. It had sat there this whole long fantastic month while I was falling in love with Tyler Oneota.

The highway ran close to the house, heading northeast from Liberal to Wichita, a flat, narrow, boring highway with rusty wire fences along it that were held up mostly by weeds and wildflowers. Then the wheat fields, the flat pastureland with its sparse little trees and tough grasses, and just here and there the roof and trees of somebody's home, plain and dusty and serviceable, like mine.

In front of me stood a small barn-shaped building, close to the road, with a parking area in front of it. A wood-burned sign over the door said "Saddle Shop." It had a wood porch with a couple of crude split-log benches and a

Coke machine that didn't go with the rustic decor at all. But it brought in a little money, so what the heck. People driving by would pull in just to use the pop machine, and sometimes they'd wander into the shop and buy something.

I could see the edge of town if I stood in my stirrups. Liberal. From here, just the beginning of the houses and a Bronco gas station. On around the circle, a jumble of rough-fenced pens and corrals, a big old barn that looked like a giant hen with all the little sheds as its chicks.

I stared up at the window of Tyler's room, hoping to see his head poking out. Just looking at his bedroom window made me love him all over again.

Impatient with my life, I spun the buckskin filly around and booted her into a lope. She was on her left lead; I could feel it in the angle of her body movement. I reined her in a left circle, then shifted my weight, shoved her hindquarters over with hard leg pressure behind the saddle, and reined her to the right.

She stumbled and nearly fell.

Damn.

I steadied her with pressure on the hackamore reins and brought her up into a right-

5

circle lope. She picked up her right-foot lead like she was supposed to, but it wasn't the flying lead change I'd been trying to teach her all summer. She'd had to stumble and almost fall in order to get herself in gear for the new direction of travel.

One more week and the guy from Tulsa would be coming through, stopping to see the buckskin filly. If she was far enough along in her training to be sure she had the ability for cutting-horse competition, he'd most likely buy her. When he called a couple of weeks ago looking for a good filly I'd told him thirty-five hundred dollars for her, and he said he was interested.

Course, I also told him she had her lead changes down pat.

Thirty-five hundred would go a long way toward Daddy's hospital bills over there in Durango. Whether they'd even let Daddy out of the hospital without their money, I had no idea. He'd been in hospitals before, naturally, being in his line of work, but never since I was old enough to be let in on the family money worries.

Welcome to adulthood, Denny Browner. Whoopee.

I had been welcomed to adulthood anyway.

Tyler saw to that. I ought to have known better than to fall for a rodeo cowboy. Listening to my daddy all these years bragging about which of his many famous lines was working with this little ole girl, or that little ole girl. Sometimes it was the lonesome line, where he told them nobody really understood him or cared for him. Or other times it was the one about how he'd been hurt so bad when his wife left him with a little girl to take care of that he just never learned to trust again . . . till now. He had a whole bunch of them, all polished to perfection.

Sometimes I couldn't help but wonder when Tyler was murmuring into my neck and unbuttoning my clothes just how much of what he was saying he had learned from hanging around with my daddy so long. But Tyler wasn't my dad. He was different.

I stripped the saddle off the filly, pulled the hackamore off over her ears, and turned her loose in the corral for a buck-run and a roll in the dust. She came up shaking herself like a wet puppy, spraying red dust up into the slanting rays of the morning sun. When she stopped shaking, there was a saddle-shaped patch of dust left sticking to her, where she'd done her most serious sweating.

When I caught her up again and hooked the rope halter around her head, she rubbed her sweat-itchy face against my body, gouging eyes and ears into my chest. Running my hand down onto the soft pads of flesh on her own chest, between her forelegs, I felt the skin cooled to normal temperature, so I let her drink a little at the trough before I turned her out with her friends in the small creek pasture behind the barn.

In the house, I washed the horse smell and dust off me as best I could at the deep old rusty sink that stood for that purpose just inside the kitchen door. Gramma B. wasn't down yet, so I went on out again and brought in the sheets off the line, folded them into big rough squares, and left them piled in the laundry basket on top of the washer. The washer and dryer shared the end of the kitchen with the chore sink, a pile of boots and egg cartons, a few cats, and a cardboard box full of green tomatoes.

Not exactly *Better Homes and Gardens*, but it was all so familiar that I barely saw it.

Gramma B. came downstairs as I was putting the coffee on. She was like the kitchen and the rest of the house—big and plain and too familiar to see clearly. She stood taller than me, but I was gaining on her. Her brown and gray hair was pulled back in a long ponytail. Her square face was the color and texture of oatmeal, with big strong features and steady eyes that could nail you to the wall if you tried to lie to her. The rest of her was shapeless and soft under her shirt and jeans. Her husband was eighteen years dead, but she still wore his clothes. Said it was like a hug from him, putting on that old blue shirt of his.

You'd never know from looking at her that she'd been out late last night hosting a lingerie party.

She shuffled across the kitchen, patting me on the shoulder and reaching for a coffee cup in the same sweep of her arm. She smelled stale and sleepy-warm.

I poured a giant bowl of Cheerios for myself, and tomato juice and coffee, and sat in my usual place at the table. Gramma B. and I talked around what was really on our minds; Tyler and Daddy on mine, who knows what on hers.

"Filly coming along?" she asked.

"Not bad. Still can't get her into her lead changes, though. She's left-footed, and she fights going onto her right lead. Fell all over herself this morning."

"She be ready, you think, by the time that guy comes to look at her?"

"Yeah, probably. Maybe. I'll keep working her."

What we *didn't* talk about was where the money was going to come from for the hospital and whatever else Daddy was going to need if that filly didn't sell.

We had fourteen head of registered quarter horses on the place at that moment; Bar B-Q, our old stallion who was almost twenty but still a working stud, four mares of various ages and quality, and a bunch of youngsters in training, some that we bred ourselves, some we bought or traded for. They'd all go, eventually, for working stock horses or for rodeo roping or cutting stock, or for pleasure horses. But the flashy buckskin filly was the only one with a hot potential buyer at the moment.

I thought about all those young horses needing regular daily work, and Tyler leaving today, and Daddy coming home in a wheelchair, which would probably be the best he could hope for for the rest of his life.

I thought about no more prize money coming in from Daddy's rodeo circuits. He and Tyler had been working up to being serious contenders for National Champion team ropers this year. Thousands of dollars in prize money for that, along with what they'd been earning all season.

And then his horse bowed a tendon, and Tyler couldn't borrow another horse with the necessary talent; so he'd come back here to develop one of Daddy's horses. And meantime, Daddy had to take on somebody else as his header, so Tyler was out of work and had to stay on here because he couldn't afford anyplace else.

Thank you, God.

And then the call last Thursday in the middle of the night. Daddy was in the hospital with a busted back; they'd be sending him home in a week because there was nothing a hospital could do for him. But that wouldn't keep them from charging a fortune.

It might or might not be permanent, the way the doctor explained it on the phone. Probably, but not for sure. Time and therapy, he said, but don't hold out much hope for anything but a wheelchair from now on.

A rodeo rider's family lives with injuries, hospitals, possibilities of death or permanent crippling; you just plain grow up with it as part of your life. It's the background, like low clouds on the horizon. Might rain later, but you do your wash anyhow. You accept it and don't think about it unless you have to.

Now it was here. It had happened to us, to Daddy. I think Gramma and I almost didn't react to it at all, or not the way we should have. It was like the inevitable that had finally come along and ended the waiting for it. I knew that later, when Daddy was really here, trying to do for himself and get around in the wheelchair, reality would hit us over and over again, gut punches. But for now it seemed as if all we could think about, in our secret thoughts, was money worries. I could read Gramma B.'s face, and she could read mine. The fact that we weren't talking about it out loud didn't mean the big worry wasn't at the breakfast table with us, big as life and twice as ugly, as Daddy was always saying.

And part of me was a little bit mad at Tyler for leaving just when I needed him. Sure, he had to get back out onto the circuit and start earning, and maybe his aim was to take over as the family breadwinner. I sure hoped so. But on the other hand, maybe not. There was always that tiny possibility that he was just plain leaving . . .

2

The first thing I ever saw of Tyler Oneota was his butt.

It was a year and a half ago, just before Christmas. Daddy came home from the Nationals with Tyler in tow like a sick puppy. Tyler was six feet tall and hard-muscled as a rock, but he was so drunk that day, Daddy had to plain out carry him into the house over his shoulder. He dumped Ty on the living room couch and said to me, "Merry Christmas, Denny. I'd 've gift wrapped him for you except he smelled so bad I couldn't get close enough to tie the bow."

As I helped Daddy straighten the guy out on the couch and pry his boots off, I could tell Daddy wasn't entirely joking. This old boy

13

stunk of everything from cheap perfume to cheap whiskey, and when the boots finally came off, I could see his socks just had a life of their own.

"Where did you get him from, the pound?" I asked.

"Honey, you don't want to know."

Gramma B. was in the kitchen, welcoming Daddy home in her usual way, with coffeepot and barbecue sandwiches. No matter what time of day or night Daddy came home from a circuit, she always had coffee and 'cues on the table within minutes.

Daddy dropped the guy's boot and picked me up for a whirling hug, grunting. "You put on a few pounds, girl. Have to work it off you. Everything okay with you?"

We didn't correspond much while he was on the road. "Yeah, okay. Who is this guy, Daddy?"

"That's Ty. He's my new partner. He ain't completely broke in yet, but he's got the makings of a fine header. He's a little under the weather at the moment."

I chuckled.

It wasn't unusual for Daddy to bring home a buddy after a rodeo trip. Some of those guys didn't have a home base to go to, and we had a spare bedroom and barn space for visiting horses. I'd never paid much attention to the others, but this one . . . he was handsome. No other word for it. Not cute, not nice looking, he was plain out handsome. His hair was long and straight and coarse, and a funny sort of dusky blond, blond shading to black rather than to brown. I'd never seen hair like it before. His features were sharp-carved, his lips full and flat, almost brown in color. He was unusually narrow-shouldered for a professional roper, but his arms, what I could see of them, were hard-muscled and corded with veins.

Looking at those veins made me want to stroke them.

I was fifteen years old. I hadn't been interested in boys since I got too old to play Show Me with the neighbor kids. Horses and my friend Sue, and the kids we ran around with from school, that was enough for me. That, and knowing what kind of guy my dad was, listening to him and his buddies talk about women. You'd think grown men would have enough sense to know that every word spoken on a porch can be heard from the window above it.

Sue and I spent quite a few interesting evenings scrunched down on the floor of the upstairs hallway under that window, learning facts of life we didn't half understand, even talking them over later in my room and trying to guess what some of the words meant.

Tyler Oneota stayed at our place for four months that winter, and I never touched him once. I'd get close, walking around behind his chair at the kitchen table or squeezing through a doorway, but he didn't touch me, and I didn't touch him. I doubt that he noticed me.

I noticed him, though.

He was there not only to sit out the off-season between rodeo circuits but also to get himself one of our horses. I never did understand the series of trades and deals that got him tied up with Daddy, but it ended up with Tyler trading off his good roping horse. He swapped the horse for a nearly new Dodge club-cab pickup with a matching two-horse trailer and tires with visible tread still on them. Daddy had just lost his roping partner, had a good horse and a barn full of promising quarter horses back home, but he didn't have transportation for himself or his horse. The marriage was made in heaven.

Every minute I wasn't in school that winter, I was on the corral fence watching those two or riding with them as they sorted through the possibilities, looking for the best roping horse for Ty.

They ended up with a four-year-old dark sorrel mare they named Sioux B-Q, a daughter of our stud and a world-champion roping mare. I knew she was Daddy's favorite of the young stock we had then. When Ty announced his choice, Daddy nodded over to me and said, "You're going to have to marry him now, Hon. I don't want to let this mare get out of the family."

They hoo-hawed and punched at each other and rode off toward the house to sign the ownership papers on the mare, leaving me red-faced and stirred up.

Sue and I watched Tyler go through three women in that four months he was with us. One worked in the cafe in town where Daddy and Tyler liked to go for coffee on their many errands here and there. One he picked up in the Roundup Bar and Grill on a very wet Saturday night, and I'm not talking rainstorm. She moved in and was all set to live in our house till Gramma B. put her foot down. The third one I never did know where he found her, but she was a ring-tailed dandy.

He turned up with her one morning and said he'd told her she could stay with us because her husband was after her with a gun. Tiffany, her name was. All wild blond hair and huge eyes, and she couldn't tell a lie from the truth even while it was coming off her tongue. Gramma wouldn't let her stay, either.

For the first part of that four months, Sue and I shared a crush on Tyler. But then, as we learned these little details about his love life from eavesdropping, Sue started turning against him. But I didn't. He had too much hold on me by then. After that I didn't talk to her as much about how I felt toward him. It was the first space to come between us since fifth grade.

Rodeo season started the end of March, and Daddy and Tyler loaded up the pickup, hitched on the trailer, and led in the horses. Daddy hugged me and swung me in his usual circle till my legs flew out behind me, but I could tell he was itching to get on the road.

Just before he got into the truck, Tyler swooped me up in the same swinging hug and planted a kiss on my mouth, right there in front of Daddy. It was the first time he'd acted like he even knew I was female.

"Hey, watch it," Daddy bellowed, and they drove away laughing and punching at each other.

They were gone for seven weeks that trip, then home again and off again through the summer. Then came the long three-month season leading up to the national championship finals, when they were rodeoing every weekend, sometimes four or five days a week, with travel time squeezed in. They, along with every other top roping team in the PRCA circuit, were pushing for qualifying points that would put them in the top ten, eligible for the championship finals. They wouldn't take any trips home till it was over. They made the finals and finished fifth, good enough to make it a profitable year.

A profitable year was any time the prize money was more than travel expenses, entry fees, and bar bills.

I spent that whole time waiting for them to come home, my Daddy and the man I'd been dreaming about all this time.

Daddy came home. Tyler didn't. He'd met some groupie at the finals and gone off home with her for a weekend that turned into the whole four months of the off-season.

That cured me. That cured me of him for good and all.

Till a month ago, when he came driving in with Sioux B-Q in the trailer and a grin on his face.

3

He was a quieter, more subdued Tyler this time around, maybe because Daddy wasn't there, maybe because his horse was hurt, I wasn't sure. Anyhow I liked him better. If that was possible.

I started playing a fantasy in my mind. I did that a lot. Mostly I didn't even tell Sue about these stories that would go on in my head. Sue never had a secret daydream in her life. I'd bet money on that. But I did, and they all had to do with some wonderful guy who was so much in love with me that he would think everything I did was perfect, and he'd never look at another woman till the day he died.

And there I was with Tyler Oneota living right in the house with me, just as if we were married. Naturally Gramma B. was there, too, but she spent most of her time in the saddle shop during the day and was off giving lingerie parties four or five nights a week.

This time around, Tyler stayed home working with the horses and tinkering with his truck. He worried over Sioux B-Q's leg, soaking it and wrapping it and squinting at her while I led her in circles.

I know he was worried about money, not being able to work without a horse. And I know he was stewing about not getting back into competition in time to qualify for the Nationals. All his quietness and worrying made him more lovable than he'd been last year.

This is the real Tyler Oneota, I told myself. This is a man worth loving, a man who could love me.

So I let the daydreams take over my mind. We were married and living here together with a mostly invisible Gramma B., and Tyler worshiped me and adored me. He'd take me with him on circuits. I knew some of the guys took their wives, not too many because of the expense, but some. Tyler and Denny Oneota.

With the daydream playing in my head, I guess I must have been giving off signals to Tyler. Body language. Sue had these theories about what you could tell about a person by how they crossed their legs or held their arms. If they crossed their arms over their chests, it was to keep other people from getting too close. Or if they were always touching you on the arm or shoulder when they talked, it meant a desire for closer contact. Or if they wouldn't look you in the eye, it was because they were afraid you would be able to read their thoughts.

Anyhow, Tyler and I started touching, a pat in passing, stuff like that. And I'd catch him looking at me sometimes. He'd stare at me and then drop a big old wink for no reason, just a message of closeness.

We spent most of our time that first week he was here going through the horses looking for one he could use while Sioux B-Q's leg healed. He figured if he could get a substitute going well enough, he could catch up with Daddy in time for the Arkansas circuit the last week of June.

One by one we caught up the broke horses, threw Ty's roping saddle on them, and gave them a try. He'd take them in the big corral and work them out, fast starts and stops, quick turns to see which ones could get down over their hocks for the fast spins. He swung his rope around their faces, slapped them all over with it, testing for steadiness, dropped a few loops over Ferdinand, the wooden-dummy steer we used for training.

When the choice was narrowed down to three, I rode with him out to the calf pasture, where we kept a dozen head of yearling steer calves for training purposes. I never did learn to rope, although I tried for hours on end when I was a little kid. I wanted Daddy to think I was good. But I plain out didn't have the wrist strength for it. Girls don't, usually. So I couldn't act as the other half of a roping team for Tyler; I could only go along and help cut a calf out of the herd for him to rope on.

Tyler was a header specialist, and my daddy was the heeler. That's what a roping team is. The two ropers come out of the chute together, just behind the steer, and the header ropes the steer's head while the heeler does the really tricky part, roping the two back feet while the steer is running and dodging for all he's worth. A heeler is a real master, let me tell you. It takes *split* split-second timing to lay a loop under that steer just when and just where those hind hooves are coming down.

I sat in my saddle, those hot June mornings, squinting against the sun and the dust and watching Tyler lean out over the neck of a racing horse, following the line of his rope with the line of his body, throwing with strength and precision. I sat and watched and fell in love. No other word for it.

In the hot part of the afternoon, we'd give it a rest and take over the saddle shop while Gramma B. went into the house to watch her soap operas and take a nap. She had her little TV in the saddle shop of course, but for her special programs she preferred a bigger screen, and color.

The shop didn't need all that much tending. If we got two or three customers in an afternoon, it was pretty good, and we could have watched from the house for cars to drive in. But it was cool and dim and leathery smelling in the shop, the pop machine was handy, and we could be alone. We liked it in there.

We'd sit all afternoon, me in the old tilting wooden desk chair behind the counter and Tyler on a big, padded-seat pleasure saddle astride a sawhorse. We'd kill off Coke after Coke, rubbing the cold sweaty cans against our wrists and temples first, for maximum chill effect.

And we'd talk. He told me about his background; his dad was half Sioux, half Irish, his mom was pure Norwegian. They'd lived in town, but he'd had friends from school who lived in the country and had horses. One friend was into high school rodeo, and from him Tyler had caught the love of the sport. He'd messed around with bronc and bull riding, decided he wasn't crazy enough for those specialties, and settled on calf roping, bulldogging, and eventually specialized in team roping with his buddy.

They'd won the regional team roping championship the last year they were eligible for high school rodeos, and his dad had backed him in his decision to make roping a career. He'd earned enough in high school to buy a ratty old pickup and trailer, and his parents went into hock to buy him a trained, talented roping horse for graduation.

He really hated having to trade that horse off for the truck and trailer, but the horse was beginning to lose that sharp competitive edge that makes a roping horse great. Sometimes they just get tired of doing it. But he was still fast enough to be worth a truck and trailer, Tyler told me, and his folks understood. His old pickup had died, his old trailer was rotten in the floorboards, and life goes on.

It was around then that he and Daddy had paired up, partly because Daddy'd had a run of bad luck and injuries and couldn't afford to keep his old truck patched together. They'd needed each other, and it had worked out great.

When he asked about my life, I didn't know what to say. I hadn't had a life yet. I told him my mom had left when I was six, probably because Daddy was playing around with everything in tight jeans west of the Mississippi. Told him she was living up in McCook, Nebraska, which was her home town. Had her own dog-grooming business up there. Told him I didn't go up to visit much anymore. She had boyfriends and a busy life. I had my life down here, and I had Gramma B. to mother me when I needed it.

I'm not sure why Tyler spent so much time in my company this last month. I'd like to believe it was because I'd blossomed into a drop-dead gorgeous fox, but more likely it was just because I was handy, or because he was burned-out on flashy groupie types, or because when he got to know me he genuinely liked me.

Came the day when Tyler set down his pop can and took me by the elbow and pulled me into his arms.

Came the night when Tyler took me by the elbow and led me into his bedroom while

Gramma B. was off selling black-lace tap pants to women who wanted to keep love alive.

Came the time when Tyler did those things with me that he probably did all the time with whatever groupies offered themselves on the road and then joked and compared notes with Daddy afterwards.

But this was different. This was me, giving something I held dear and precious for the first time ever. It meant something to me. It meant a whole hell of a lot to me. Pretty soon now I'd find out what it meant to him.

He might tell me he loved me and wanted to marry me and take me with him on the circuit. He might say he loved me and wanted us to write letters every day and get married sometime in the future. He might promise to be faithful while he was on the road.

Or he might swing off down the road and not say anything about that precious gift I'd given him.

In the next hour or so, I'd know.

4

Gramma B. and I both stiffened a little when Tyler started clomping down the stairs. We'd heard him in the bathroom while we ate our silent breakfasts, heard him singing while he shaved, heard the nasal twang of his song while he pinched off his nose to shave under it.

He came into the kitchen smelling of Stetson aftershave and looking so beautiful I had to turn away. It was like Sue's theories; if I'd looked him in the eye, he'd have seen my love for him, and so would Gramma B.

She was edgy, this morning, clanking her spoon too loud in her coffee cup and fiddling with the channels on the little TV that sat on the table. It was already on the morning show she always watched, but she went all the way around the dial and ended up on the same channel.

"What time you want to be on the road?" I asked Tyler.

"Soon's I can. Stillwater's a good six-hour drive. I should have got up early and been there before the heat of the day."

He was avoiding looking at me, too. Maybe he, too, didn't want his love to show in front of Gramma B.

"So how was it last night?" he asked in a sudden, loud voice.

I looked up, frozen by his question.

Last night? Last night we made love in his bed in the guest room, me putting everything I had into it, hoping to pull the love words out of him. The commitment.

But he was talking to Gramma B., smiling at her.

"Fine," she said. "Sold that lavender gown and robe set, you remember, the hundred-eighty-nine dollar one with the black lace? Sold a couple of the baby doll sets, and the red teddy with the heart-shaped cutouts."

Tyler grinned. "That one always was my favorite. Who'd you sell it to, Gramma? I'll go look her up."

"I wouldn't tell you that. You know better. Time you got on the road if you're going to start talking like that."

Tyler and Gramma and I had had fun one afternoon looking through her selection of Starlite Lingerie samples. We'd held the different pieces up to ourselves, laughing at how they looked against a cowboy, a tough old lady like Gramma B., and me.

Gramma used to sell Tupperware, but then the area got pretty well saturated with Tupperware. Everybody we knew had been to so many parties and given so many parties that there was just no place to go in the plastic bowl business.

But Gramma liked the parties, liked going out at night to be with a living room full of laughing, joking women. For Gramma it was a change from the isolation of the farmhouse; for the rest of them, probably a chance for a night out with the gals, to offset their husbands' nights out in the beer joints or bowling alleys. They'd come from all over.

When the Tupperware thing was wrung dry, she went to costume jewelry parties, then to cosmetics parties. They, in turn, hit the burn-out stage. It was mostly the same women time after time at these parties, and you can buy only so much of that stuff, even as a price for an evening out.

So Gramma answered an ad in the back of a magazine and became the Liberal, Kansas, representative for the Starlite Lingerie Company. At first I thought it was fun, looking through the samples and imagining wearing that stuff for the man I loved. But it wasn't me. Most of the women who bought it were married and working at hanging onto their husbands any way they could.

My personal feeling was that a man who needed blacklace see-through stuff before he'd stay home and be faithful wasn't worth the investment. But, at least for now, the lingerie parties kept Gramma going out nights and having a good time. And she usually cleared thirty bucks or so in commissions, so more power to her, I thought.

Tyler wolfed down a cup of coffee and a couple of pieces of toast, ran back upstairs for his bags, and was at the door while I was still rehearsing the good-bye scene.

Yesterday he'd washed the truck and trailer and shined them up. They stood, hitched and ready, beside the barn with three bales of hay, a sack of sweet feed, and Tyler's tack in the back of the truck.

Sioux B-Q stood tied in the barn, groomed and waiting. Her leg had healed faster than Ty had been able to school the best of our horses in what it would have to know to be as good as Sioux B-Q. And without a top-notch, smart, athletic, experienced horse, you can kiss top money good-bye in the cutthroat competition of world-class team roping.

I tagged after Ty, pulled the pins that let down the trailer's tailgate ramp, stood aside while he led Sioux B-Q up into the trailer. He didn't bother to tie her; she was an old hand at trailer travel and was already at work on the hay net before he slammed up the tailgate and bolted it home.

This was it. Here it came.

He threw his bags into the back of the pickup and closed the hatch on the topper. Then he walked past me to the driver's door and opened it. At last, finally at last, he turned and looked at me.

He was so damned beautiful standing there in the morning light. His hair was slicked back and behaving, for once. His skin was tanned that odd dusky-gold shade that no one else had, blending Indian and Norwegian in one skin. He wore a faded red T-shirt with a PRCA emblem almost washed off it and its short sleeves rolled up to hold his cigarettes.

There were those knotty, corded, silky arms I'd fallen in love with first. The hair on them was a funny mixture, too, harsh black masculine hairs but also a fuzz of fine gold ones that caught the sun and made something glowing out of him.

I reached out and stroked his forearm, like stroking down a horse's leg only silkier.

He pulled me in for a kiss. "You tell your Daddy I was sorry I couldn't stay to see him when he gets home. Explain about my getting this chance to team with A.J. for Stillwater."

"He'll understand," I said. My voice sounded weak.

"Well, best be on my way," he said again and put one foot in the truck. "So long, Denny. You be good now."

"Too late for that," I snapped.

His saying "So long, Denny," like that broke something in me. What I hadn't wanted to see, this whole month, was hitting me in the face in those three words. I wasn't any more to him than some handy female to kill time with. Easier than going to town looking for a bar pickup. I'd known all along that my daddy was that way, but I'd swore to myself that Ty was different. Better than that.

And behind the big knife in the back was the little scary thought—what if I was pregnant?

He came back to me then, cupped his hand around the back of my neck, and looked me in the eye for the first time all morning. His lips worked, like he was wanting to say something, but nothing came out.

"You're a good kid," he said finally. "You'll come up with somebody better than me. And listen, don't tell your daddy . . . about us . . . will you? I don't want him thinking bad of me."

"What if I'm pregnant, Tyler?"

"You're not. We were careful."

"Careful don't always do the trick, does it? Accidents happen. What if I'm carrying a little accident around inside me right now?"

He sobered for a moment. "Now, honey, you know I'd take care of you if that happened, but it didn't. It won't. We were careful."

"But what if, Tyler? You talk about taking care of me, but you're saying it with one foot on the gas pedal."

Something behind his eyes pulled away from

me, shut me out. I was pushing him, and he didn't like it. He was making the rules here, and I could either play his way or not at all.

He got into the truck and drove off without a backward wave; the game was over. The last I saw of him was his silky arm out the window, his hand slapping the roof of the cab in rhythm with his radio.

5

I could almost see the pain rolling at me like a thunderhead blowing across the sky. It scared me. I stood in the lane by the mailbox, watching that horse trailer disappear up the highway, and I just froze in dread of what I was going to feel next.

One time I cut myself deep, with a razor blade, trying to open a carton. I didn't feel the cut, but I knew the blood and the pain were going to be awful in another second. And they were. And this was just like that time.

I didn't know if I could stand the feelings that were rushing at me.

Instinct finally got me moving. I ran into the house, skinned off my jeans and shirt and replaced them with my swimsuit, then pulled the jeans on again and the shirt, unbuttoned and flapping.

Gramma B. didn't say anything, just held out her car keys to me as I came through the kitchen. Her face was still, but I could read behind it a wealth of understanding. I could have bawled right then, and she would have been sweet to me. But that wasn't really what I needed.

I drove into town, up the shady side street to the municipal swimming pool, parked and went inside.

It was Sue I needed now.

I waved in passing to the woman selling tickets.

"Don't you go in that water." She grinned. She always let me in free. She knew I was there mainly to talk to Sue, not to get a free swim. Sue pretty much got to do what she wanted at the pool since her dad donated the land for it when the pool was built.

I looked up at the clock as I went through the girls' dressing room, skinning out of my jeans and shirt as I went and leaving them over a bench. It was just after nine. Sue's classes were over by now, and she was on lifeguard duty. Perfect timing.

From eight to nine she taught Red Cross swimming lessons to little kids, and Waterbaby classes one day a week for infants and toddlers. After nine she was on lifeguard duty four days a week. Nights she had the use of the pool for her own workouts.

Water was for her what the horses were for me.

Sometimes I wondered why we ever chose each other as best friends. We had started gravitating toward each other in about fourth or fifth grade, mostly because our minds seemed to work on the same wavelength even though our interests were different.

Her mom was a high school teacher, senior English and American lit. Her dad sold real estate and had done right well for himself picking up choice bits before they came on the market and developing them or somehow figuring out the most profitable thing to do with them. The land where the pool was he'd gotten for next to nothing because of the zoning, donated it to the city for a huge tax break, and then built a Taco Bell right across from it.

So, needless to say, Sue and I were in different levels of society, but we didn't care. She thought my strange family was neat, and I thought her walk-in closet was neat, and we didn't waste energy being jealous.

It didn't matter whose family was richer. The main thing was that we felt one another's hurts, and our feelings were genuine. Nothing fake about them.

When we were fourteen, Sue's cat died. Sue got Sylvester when she was too young to remember, even, and he slept on her bed every night of her life. He wasn't much to look at, kind of a gray tiger stripe but with a dirty yellowish brown cast to his coat. But he was one of those cats that turned to rubber when you pick them up. He loved to be carried around and held and tummy-rubbed. When we were younger, we'd dress him up in doll clothes. We set him up on my horse's saddle and took pictures of him. That cat would let us do anything with him just for the pleasure of being with us. He was a rare cat.

When he died, Sue's mom said philosophical things about what a nice long life Sylvester had had. Her dad didn't say anything to us, but we heard him say to her mom, "Now maybe we can get rid of that stinking litter box."

I was the one who grieved with Sue. I helped her through it because I knew enough, and cared enough, not to talk about how he'd had a full life and it was time for him to go. I bawled right along with her, and we talked for hours about Sylvester's cute ways of doing things. And after a while we came out the other side of the grief and went on from there.

I remember another time. We were in seventh grade, and we had a bunch of about six or seven other kids that we ran around with. One of them made a remark about my daddy. He'd got his tail in a crack about that time, messing around with a married woman from over at Kismet.

She'd stopped by our place one day looking for a flashy quarter horse that she could show in pleasure classes. She was one of those women who look as if their tight jeans are choking them to death, and the buttons are always popping open on the crest of their blouses. Well, my daddy wasn't the man to resist an invitation like that woman was putting out.

I never did get the straight of the story, being too young to hear such things . . . unless they were being discussed on the front porch with the hall window open upstairs. But it had to do with her husband catching them in a tack room somewhere and pitching a sixty-pound stock saddle at Daddy's head and then throwing Daddy's pants in a stall with a stallion so mean nobody but his owner could get near him.

It was a pretty funny story for a small town, so of course it got told and told and TOLD, and who knows how much of it was true.

But the kids got hold of it, naturally, and they started in on me, making snotty remarks about my daddy tomcatting with a married woman.

I was just crushed. Here I thought these kids were my friends and that they liked me as much as I liked them. What they were doing to me was lots worse than what Daddy did. To me it was, anyhow, because it put me on the outside of the bunch when I'd always felt like I was one of the main insiders.

But then, Sue to the rescue. She was magnificent. She reared up on her hind legs and told those kids off, just ripped them up one side and down the other. She had one good point in her argument, and she kept hitting them over the head with it till they all had to agree with her: we can't none of us control what our parents do. So therefore we can't none of us be held responsible for it or take blame for it. And we shouldn't have to be teased over it by our best friends.

We all got closer after that speech of hers. We sort of looked around at one another, and it was as if we suddenly realized we had the power to hurt one another, or not to, and it was up to us to see that we all got kind treatment from our own group, no matter what the rest of the world did to us. We're still all good friends, except the ones that moved away.

The sun glared on the cement around the swimming pool, and I could smell the chlorine and hear the yells and splashes of a dozen kids. It wouldn't get crowded till later. I dove in and swam across to the base of the guard tower and pulled myself up the steps, shaking wet hair and blowing drops off my face.

Sue called it her eagle's nest up there. It was about four feet square, with a hard wooden chair and a sun roof over it. If she needed to save a drowning swimmer, she could dive straight down into the deep end of the pool.

She was almost as tall as me, but with very short, straight, tan-streaked hair and a nose that was always peeling. Her neck and shoulders were thick with the muscling of a serious swimmer, her arms and legs made of long, hard muscle. Her body was as lean and flat as a fourteen-year-old boy's. She'd given up hope of having much of anything in the way of boobs and didn't seem to care.

"Hi," she said, looking at me carefully. That one syllable was loaded with questions, with tenderness.

I just looked at her and blew upward toward my hair. She must have read despair in my eyes because hers softened and deepened.

"He's gone, huh."

"Yep," I said, and turned to watch the swimmers.

"What did he say?"

"He said, 'So long.' "

"Damn," Sue said softly.

It was the right thing to say.

I sat on the edge of the platform with my legs dangling, my head just touching her leg, while the thunderhead of pain and loss rolled over me.

A couple of tears got away from me, but my face was wet from swimming, so they probably didn't show.

Sue knew they were there, though.

Tuesday, July 11

1

I folded in my lips and blew a whistle that was shrill and breathy at the same time. "Sunny," I called.

Sun B-Q ambled toward me through an early morning haze that meant a steaming day later on. The others in the creek pasture came, too, out of optimism.

I rewarded Sunny with a handful of oats mixed with lint from my jeans pocket. She didn't mind the lint. Shooing the others back, I led the buckskin filly to the corral fence, where my saddle waited. She was in a good mood this morning, cocking her ears at the barn cats and following me pleasantly.

I brushed her down so she wouldn't get saddle acne from the sand in her coat irritating her skin when I rode her. The pasture soil was sandy, and the horses had a regular wallowing place where they'd roll and dust themselves. It helped protect their skin from the flies and bots.

I didn't have a specific horse of my own. I knew lots of kids at school who were horse nuts, and they thought I was crazy not to have one special horse all my own. I used to.

I had a little black-and-white pinto, the kind we called an Indian pony, bigger than a pony but small for a horse. Daddy got him for me when I was eight or nine, and I rode him all over the countryside and all over town for six years, long past the time my legs were too long for him. Arrow, his name was, for the arrow-shaped white spot over his rump. He'd do anything for me. I'd ride him up the steps of the Catholic church, just showing off. He'd follow me up onto the porch of our house, and he'd have followed me inside if Gramma hadn't had a fit.

He was such a neat horse. If little kids rode him, he was just as quiet and safe as could be, but if some wise-ass boy from school got on him and started cowboying around on him, old Arrow would unload the kid faster than scat. When Sue rode him, hanging onto the saddle horn every step of the way, he never put a foot wrong. She loved him almost as much as I did. And when I rode him, he'd give me as much speed and spirit as I wanted.

He died of a twisted gut about a month after Sue's cat, Sylvester, died. It was Sue's idea for us to bury Arrow like we buried Sylly-cat, even though it meant her and me spending one entire day digging a hole big enough. We both had shovel blisters that lasted two weeks. We got a neighbor to come over with his tractor and front-loader and haul Arrow to his grave in the creek pasture. And later Sue helped me make a grave marker with her wood-burning set.

There was never going to be another Arrow in my heart, not for a long time after that. I just started spreading my love in a thin layer over the dozen or so horses Daddy was breeding and raising. That way, when one got sold, it hardly left a dent in me. And as I got older and more aware of money worries, I got so I could positively rejoice at seeing a horse of ours going off in somebody else's trailer.

Right now, with Daddy crippled and God only knows what medical expenses facing us, my main job was to get Sunny taking her lead changes in time for the Tulsa guy to buy her. No time to think about Daddy in a wheelchair.

No need to think about Tyler Oneota driving away with my virginity notched up on his scorecard.

No. Just think about the damn horse.

I swung on board and worked the filly at a jog around the corral until she settled down and started paying attention. There was a curve in her spine that I could feel through the saddle, telling me she'd buck if I let her lope.

We worked both ways around the circle, turning and stopping and backing, until her spine leveled out.

Then we loped in an easy rocking stride around the ring both ways, doing big circle turns in both directions. She wanted to keep on her left lead even on the right turns, and she'd trip herself most times.

Finally, when she was limbered up enough, I put her into a big roomy figure-eight, circling left for a full round. In the center, I slowed her to a trot for two strides, then started in a lope in the other direction. She picked up her right lead and made the turn perfectly.

Back at the center point, I broke her lope down to a trot just for one stride and set her out again, left circle, left lead. She did it.

Coming around again to the center point, I

held my breath, reined, and legged her over into the right-hand circle.

She stumbled.

Damn.

Again and again we tried for the flying lead change. Every time she broke down to a trot or stumbled. Or bucked.

When she started bucking and fighting me on it, I knew it was time to hang it up for the day. You can only push a young horse so far without doing more harm than good.

Sometimes I wasn't entirely sure I had the patience to be a horse trainer. Daddy said I was good at it, and I wanted to think so, but sometimes I'd get so frustrated I'd almost boil over. Here I'd been working with Sunny for the better part of a month, trying to get her to take that flying change, and she didn't seem any closer to it now than she was when we started. Day after day, repeat after repeat, and circle after circle, and she couldn't seem to get the idea of what I wanted. I knew from past experience that if I kept at it, there'd come a turning point in her mind and she'd do it right, and after that it'd come easy, but there was no way of knowing when that turning point would happen. Might be tomorrow, might be next month, after the Tulsa guy had come and gone and bought somewhere else. Daddy used to keep reminding me that training horses was like growing trees; you got results eventually but nothing happened very fast.

I turned her out and went after the next colt on my work schedule.

Again, as I had over and over the past few days, I wondered what it was going to be like when Daddy came home. Was he really going to be paralyzed from the hips down for the rest of his life? That was what it had sounded like when we talked to him and the doctor on the phone. Daddy himself hadn't said much about it, only that he'd be home as soon as they'd let him out and that he reckoned Hoyt or one of the other guys would fly him back.

If Daddy was out of the rodeoing profession, and it sure looked that way, could we make a living just with the saddle shop and our few head of quarter horses? Would I have to quit school and miss my senior year in order to take care of things here? It was a real possibility, or at least it looked that way from where I stood.

And what would Daddy be like, in a wheelchair? If he wasn't on the back of a horse or chasing some woman, he wouldn't hardly be recognizable as Daddy, would he?

As awful as Daddy's situation was, it couldn't keep my mind from slipping off toward Tyler. Yesterday I'd come home from the pool, worked like a son of a gun all day on the horses, riding every one of them including old Bar B-Q who hadn't been rode in three years. If I slowed down, Tyler would catch up with my mind and drive me nuts. After supper I went along with Gramma on one of her parties, and laughed and hoo-hawed along with all those gals trying on all those skimpy sexy under-things.

But Tyler was gaining on me this morning. I couldn't keep my mind away from Stillwater, Oklahoma, where he was competing today with his new roping partner. Being looked at by all those groupies who hang out at rodeos just asking to be picked up.

I caught up the roughest of the two-year-olds, and I worked the legs right off her I was so mad at Tyler Oneota for dumping me.

Mad at Denny Browner for walking into it, throwing her heart on the bed just like she didn't have good sense. Letting herself be had.

Damn!

2

Sue smelled like pool chlorine even on her day off. We sat in the saddle shop with its fragrance of leather and neat's-foot oil, and still, if I closed my eyes, I'd think I was at the pool, the chlorine-sharpness was so clear in the air. It was in her hair, I think. Sometimes in summer her hair would get a faint greenish tinge to it when the sun hit it. From the chlorine. She liked it that way. Swimmers' hair, she called it.

There had been a time last spring when there was a space in our togetherness, as that poet, what's-his-name, said. Gibran, was that the guy? He said there should be spaces in the togetherness of lovers because two pillars standing close together couldn't support as much weight as two pillars standing apart.

Of course Sue and I weren't lovers, but it was probably true for best friends, too, since the relationships had quite a bit in common.

Before last spring the only apartness we had was in my mind, when I'd been so crazy about Tyler that first time around and Sue had cooled on him. We were still as good friends as ever, but there was that one subject we stayed off of, and for me it was a pretty big hole to waltz around because he was on my mind all the time.

Then, about the time I was getting over him this past spring, Sue made an out-of-the-blue announcement that she was going out on a date. With Norman from the swim team. I never even knew she was interested in Norman or any other guy. It was a total shock to me.

The worst of it was that Norman was very nice. If I was picking out a boyfriend for Sue, he'd probably be my choice. He was as interested in swimming as she was, he was nice enough looking, smart enough, sweet and thoughtful, everything you'd want for your best friend's boyfriend.

But what hurt was that I was left out of the whole thing. She never told me she wanted to go out with him, never told me he'd been working up to asking her at swim team practices, nothing. Just all of a sudden, they were dating. Before that, we told each other everything we thought and felt about every kid at school.

They only went out together four or five times, right around the end of the school year. But it meant that Sue had a date for the prom, and I went with three other girls who didn't have dates. In our school that's no big thing; probably half the kids don't have actual dates for the proms. But Sue did. And that hurt a little bit.

Then after school got out, they quit going out together. All I could get out of Sue was a shrug and, "It just didn't work out," in such an offhand tone that I honestly think she lost interest in him. Or they lost interest in each other at the same time.

But there again, she should have been telling me everything.

I told her everything when it started up again between me and Tyler. I couldn't help myself. I had to have somebody to tell it to, and she was the one I trusted completely.

I felt as though her not confiding in me about Norman meant that she was a stronger person than I was. Able to keep secrets. I didn't like that feeling.

But it didn't keep me from spilling my guts to her that afternoon in the saddle shop. She had beat me to the one chair, behind the cash register, but I was just as comfortable in the saddle on the sawhorse. It was one of those super-soft jobs, with the quilted suede seat . . . and it was where Tyler always used to sit.

"Look at it this way," Sue was saying. "He was only here a month. He didn't get to be so much of a habit in your daily life that it's going to take you forever to get back into your old routine. And listen, if he'd been worthy of you, he wouldn't have dumped you. That's our standard theory."

"I know. I remember when we made up that rule for ourselves. What were we, seventh grade, eighth grade? When we were talking about how can you tell if you're in love, and what about if you're in love with somebody and he doesn't love you back. And we decided that it wasn't going to be a problem because if they didn't love us, that meant they weren't good enough for us and we wouldn't love them in the first place. Wasn't that how it went?"

Sue grinned. She had very large white teeth, like Chiclets gum.

"That's right. If we stick to that rule, we'll

never get our hearts broken, old buddy. Will we?"

"Yes, but we left out an important fact that we probably didn't even know about back then. You can't *help* who you fall in love with."

"Yes you can. You didn't really love Tyler, Denny, you know you didn't. You had the hots for his body, and that was understandable. But you didn't have any real closeness with him, not where it counts." She tapped the side of her head.

"Well, that's true in a way."

"And you knew he was a hell-raiser with women. I mean you knew that going into it, didn't you?"

"Oh sure. But yet, I don't know, he seemed different this summer. More settled down, you know? He never looked at another woman while he was here."

She snorted and kicked gently at my foot. "He didn't have to. He had all the comforts of home, at home, and without your dad in the way."

I just shook my head. This hurt too much to talk about, so casually, so soon. I stared away from Sue, at the row of feather hatbands hanging from the ceiling, and blinked back the tears.

"Sorry," Sue murmured. "Open mouth, insert foot. I don't mean to be rubbing salt, kid. I just have the feeling that it's not actually Tyler that you're grieving for so much as, you know, what you gave him."

I sighed. "It comes down to the same thing, in a way. I gave him a whole lot more than he gave me, you know? In emotion. I'm not talking about virginities here, I'm talking about how much I cared about him, versus how much he cared about me. Being . . . took . . . like that makes me feel, I don't know. Worthless. Like he saw more of me than anybody else has ever seen, and I didn't measure up.

"I keep thinking about how I was, in bed, and how I stacked up against all those other women he's had, and it just seems clear that I wasn't very good at it. At making love. If I'd been better, he wouldn't have dumped me. I know I'm not a terribly feminine type and all that, but I felt like I had some valuable things to give a guy. Warmth and honesty and stuff like that. Now, I don't know if I'd have the courage to get that close to another guy. I'd be afraid of flunking the test again. Getting dumped again. You know?"

"I know what you're saying, but I think

you're missing the whole point, which is that Tyler Oneota isn't worth the dirt on your boots, and you're better off getting him out of your system and getting on with your life. *Comprende?*"

She kicked me again, and I had to smile a little.

A pickup pulled up outside. We turned to see if it was anybody we knew. He was a beefy, middle-aged guy spilling out over the top of his jeans. He stopped at the pop machine first, then came into the shop. He was a fairly regular customer, but I couldn't remember his name.

"Howdee," he called, raising his Dr. Pepper in greeting. "I just want to look at these here fleece saddle pads. Don't get up. I can find what I want. Nice and cool in here. Them fans of yours really do a job, don't they? Hotter than the hubs of hell out there today. All that humm-ditity. I'm sorry to hear about Doe's accident. How's he doing? Still in the hospital is he?"

The man set his pop can on top of the display of belt buckles and began sorting through the stack of fleece saddle pads.

I got down from the saddle I'd been sitting

on and went over to him. There was a 50 percent markup on those saddle pads, a clear profit of ten bucks or so.

"Here," I said, "these in this stack are square-cornered and double thickness; these here are the plaids or solid colors on one side, fleece on the other, and you can use them either way; and then these over here are the rounded ones, for your rounded-skirt saddles."

He pulled one from a stack, looked it over, and nodded. "This'll do the trick. And a can of that good three-in-one leather cleaner, and a *Stock Horse Journal* if you got the July issue. How is your daddy?" he asked again.

"He's still in the hospital at Durango. That's twenty-seven thirty with tax. Should be home later this week. They were talking like it's permanent damage to the main nerves to his legs. He may be in a wheelchair permanently."

"Aw, that's a shame. Poor old Doe. What the hell was he doing climbing around on bucking chutes at two in the morning, anyway?"

I stared at him.

He looked suddenly confused. "Didn't you know how he got hurt?"

I shook my head. "All they said when they called from the hospital was that he had a fall at the rodeo grounds. What *was* he doing up on the bucking chutes?"

I handed the man his sack. He took it and headed for the door, swiping his Dr. Pepper can as he went.

"Damned if I know. The story I heard was that he was stringing ladies' underthings over the time clock. But I expect that wasn't true. Y'all have a good day now, hear?"

The door slammed behind him.

Sue and I stared at each other.

3

Gramma B. and I were just finishing up supper, with an empty evening in front of us. No Starlite party on the schedule. We were sitting at the table and debating whether it would be worth the effort to drive into town for a movie. We'd decided it wasn't worth the money or the effort when we could sit home and watch TV for nothing.

My only reason for suggesting it in the first place was restlessness, left over from Tyler. I had to get back into the groove of evenings with Gramma B. again, instead of with him, and a movie seemed like it might help get me past this one evening anyhow.

But in the talks Gramma and I had had about money since we got the call about Daddy's accident, we'd pretty much decided to see if we couldn't live on what the saddle shop brought in, at least for our daily expenses, food and utilities and whatnot. Today's profit from the shop was maybe fifteen bucks. Using eight of that for a movie neither of us much wanted to see didn't make sense.

I'd have to work out my Tyler blues some other way.

That other way presented itself just about the time we were sighing and heaving ourselves up from the table to shift the dirty dishes to the sink.

A car door slammed outside.

We looked out the window over the sink and saw that it was a dusty little hatchback, parked by the house, not by the shop, and a woman was getting out.

"I'll be dipped in goose grease," Gramma said under her breath. "It's that woman! What in hell is she doing here?"

"What woman?"

"Rita, you fool. Don't you even recognize your own mama?" Gramma sounded madder than hell. Not at me, I knew that. At the woman getting out of the car.

My mama? I stared, slack-jawed, out the window. My mama?

I'd almost forgotten about her. God, what a

thing to admit, but it was true! I hadn't seen her for years, hadn't had anything but birthday cards from her in all that time, and a present at Christmas. Never anything I had any use for.

Now, here she was, not only getting out of a car in our yard but hauling three suitcases out after her.

"Lord deliver me, she's landing on us!" Gramma leaned toward the window screen and yelled: "Don't you bother getting them suitcases out of your car, miss; you ain't staying in my house."

I was already slamming out the door and running toward her.

But I stopped a little ways away, suddenly not knowing what to do or say, not even recognizing this person except . . . yes, now that I saw her up close, she was my mama.

Her hair was so different. It was a huge wild bush of sort of reddish brown frizz. It made her thin little face look that much thinner and littler. She had fake-looking black eyebrows painted on, and two shades of purple eyeshadow, dark red thin lips, and dark wrinkled throat skin, like she'd overdone herself at the tanning parlor.

"Denny, baby," she cried, and flung her

arms around me. "My God, girl, I didn't hardly recognize you. You've got so big. You're half a head taller than me already, and you're only sixteen."

"Seventeen, Mama."

"What?"

"I'm seventeen. What are you doing here? Why didn't you call and tell us you were coming?"

She stood up away from me, kind of tall and proud, although she wasn't much more than five feet. She wore white jeans with flowers embroidered all over them, and a big loose top like a Mexican serape. That and the flowered jeans and the hairdo added up to . . . a sight to behold.

"I came to take care of y'all," she said. "Your daddy called me from the hospital and told me about his terrible accident and how he's going to be crippled maybe permanently, so naturally I came as soon as I could close up my grooming shop and get down here. What's a mama for, anyway, am I right?"

"Right," I said vaguely. "Wait a minute, you mean Daddy called you and asked you to move back in with us?"

"Well, not exactly asked, but I know it was

what he wanted. He's going to need a lot of tending, and I'm here to do it."

"But, Mama . . ."

"Here, take this bag. And this one. Can you get this one, too? There you go. I've got a couple of houseplants in here, and of course Muffy."

She dove into the car one last time and came up with pots of trailing plants in one arm, and an ugly little dog in the other.

From the kitchen window Gramma B. yelled, "I said never mind unloading that car, missy. You're not welcome in my house."

"That's why I didn't call ahead," Mama confided as we started toward the kitchen door. "I didn't want to give your gramma time to get her guns loaded."

She marched into the house as bold as brass, with me banging through the doors behind her with the luggage.

Of course Gramma didn't have any guns; that remark was meant figuratively. But Gramma stood hard and stiff against the sink, glaring down at Mama, and if looks could kill, there would have been one dead poodle-groomer lying at our feet.

Mama set the houseplants on the counter

and lowered the dog to the floor. It was a fat, squatty little poodle, dirty cream in color, with long red tear-stains below its bugging eyes. It looked up at me and lifted its lips, threatening me with its yellow teeth.

"Hi, puppy," I said weakly. Anything for peace.

"Now look here, Barbara," Mama said to Gramma B. "We might just as well get this settled right here and now. You know well and good that Doe and I never got divorced. I am still his legal wife, this is his legal home, and you can't do a damn thing about it if I wish to come back here to care for my crippled husband."

I never saw Gramma so red-faced with fury. "No, *you* look here. I was in this house forty years before you came along. My husband and I made our home here and raised our boys in this house, and it's mine. You had it for seven years, and then you took off and left it back to me, the house and your husband and your girl. I been taking care of everybody and everything all the rest of that time, and I'll go right on ahead with the job. So you can just load up them bags and them weeds and that ratty little dog, and get yourself back into that car and head on out of here."

Mama stared at Gramma. Gramma stared back. Muffy made a puddle under the table.

Abruptly Mama turned to me and said, "Have you got a dish, darlin'? Muffy needs some water. Never mind about that puddle. I'll clean it up. She's been in the car all day, poor little thing. I've got her food and dishes out in the trunk. I'll get them in a minute, but if you could get her a drink now . . . ?"

She took two of the suitcases from my arms and marched past Gramma, toward the stairs. "I'll just put my things in Doe's room. I expect we'll have to fix him up a place downstairs, where it'll be handier. Your room, I expect, Barb. We can get started on that tomorrow. Hooeee, I need a bath. Air conditioner on my car kept cutting out on me. Darlin', have you got a cold beer in the fridge?"

Her voice disappeared up the stairs.

4

I stood in the middle of the living room, not knowing which one of them to follow, my mama upstairs singing away in Daddy's room, or Gramma slamming things in her room.

Our house was just mainly four square rooms downstairs, with doors connecting them all so you could run a whole racecourse circle through them if you were a little kid or a silly dog. The stairway made a core in the center of the four rooms, going up to a narrow hallway upstairs, and three bedrooms and bathroom up there. It was an old house, about eighty years old, very plain and a little bit slanty-floored. The woodwork around the doors was carved with grooves, though, and the glass in the front door was oval instead of square, so it did have a little bit of quality to it. It was built as a substantial farmhouse, not just some cheap throw-together little place.

The kitchen was mostly yellow and brown linoleum and wallpaper, and it was usually pretty messy. Neither Gramma nor I was much bothered by dirty dishes in the sink.

The dining room had a big table in the middle, but I couldn't remember the last time we ate on it. It was a dumping place for boxes of Starlite Lingerie, school books, bridles in need of cleaning, whatever.

The living room was just like everybody else's living room, a couch and three chairs, TV in the corner, and that was about it.

The fourth room was Gramma's, and it was a whole other world. Besides the bed and dresser and nightstand, it had all of Grampa's stuff. Over the bed was a six-foot-wide pair of longhorn horns mounted on a leather plaque. A buffalo hide rug took up every inch of floor space. On the dresser stood a horse's hoof, a genuine horse's hoof, shellacked and hollowed out to hold pens and paper clips and stuff. It was off of Grampa's favorite stock horse who died at the age of thirty. Grampa was all for having that horse stuffed and mounted, but Gramma put her foot down on that. The shellacked hoof was their compromise.

In the eighteen years since Grampa died, Gramma B. put a slight covering of herself over the room. Her nightgown hung from one tip of the steer horns and her bathrobe from the other, so they made a kind of curtain at the sides of the bed. She'd put a blue rag rug on top of the buffalo hide, beside the bed, so she didn't have to feel that hairy old thing with her bare feet. But she'd never gotten rid of the stuff. I guess it was like wearing Grampa's shirts, like a hug from him.

This room was the logical place to put Daddy when he came home from the hospital. Gramma B. and I had already more or less decided that. We just hadn't gotten around to doing anything about it yet. I knew she didn't want to move upstairs. This room had been hers and Grampa's for so long.

But what she really hated was Mama coming in here and telling her to do what she knew she had to do. I could feel all that anger coming at me through the slammed bedroom door.

I opened it and went in.

Gramma was in the little half bathroom that was tucked under the stairs, between her room and the kitchen. She came out with her toothbrush and Colgate tube in one hand, her hairbrush and comb in the other.

She tossed them into the overnight bag that was open on the bed and turned to glare at me. "I'm going over to Ranger's for the night. Call and tell them I'm on my way—I'm too mad to talk on the phone."

"What are you going over there for? Just because Mama came?"

"You said it, kiddo. I won't spend a night under the same roof as that woman. Letting her dog pee under our kitchen table where we eat our meals, for God's sake!"

She jerked so hard at her nightgown that the whole mounted steer horn pulled down from the wall and fell across the pillows.

"Now look at what she's made me do," Gramma bellowed. There was a glittering of wet in her eyes, so I didn't dare say it wasn't Mama's fault the steer horns fell off the wall.

The mood she was in, it was probably just as well she was going to Uncle Ranger's for the night.

She threw a pair of her giant-sized panties into the bag and zipped it shut.

"You call over at Ranger's and tell them I'm coming," she said again as she stomped through the living room. "I'll be back home in time to fix breakfast in the morning, and that woman had better be gone by then. You see to it that she is, Denny. And clean up that mess before we all die of food poisoning."

She waved toward the puddle under the table.

The screen door slammed. Car door slammed. Engine roared, and gravel spattered against the visiting hatchback. That was probably on purpose.

Whew.

I ripped off a handful of paper towels and took care of the dog puddle, then took the phone off the wall by the fridge and dialed Uncle Ranger's number.

Can you imagine any man insisting on naming his sons Adobe and Ranger? Well, I guess when you look at that bedroom, it's not all that surprising.

"Hi, Aunt Louise? Denny. Listen, Gramma B. is on her way over to your place. She wanted me to call and tell you."

"What's she calling ahead for? This ain't the Liberal Hilton." Aunt Louise never had a straight answer for anything. She'd had to quit going to funerals. She couldn't control her sense of humor and was always offending the bereaved.

"Well, maybe it is the Liberal Hilton. She's coming over for the night. My mama's back."

"Lord love a duck, girl. What's Rita doing back in town?"

I lowered my voice and cupped my hand around the phone. "She says she's moving back in here, to take care of Daddy when he gets out of the hospital. Gramma B. hit the ceiling. Ordered Mama out of the house. Didn't do any good. She was so mad, she pulled the steer horns down off the wall. Be prepared."

Aunt Louise laughed, and when she laughed, it came all the way up from her toes. "Hell, I thought this was going to be a boring summer. Okay, now, okay, let's get serious here. We've got some chocolate-chip ice cream. That'll help settle her down. I know what. I'll buy one of them black lace hoo-diddlies she's peddling. That'll smooth her feathers out if anything will."

"She said she'd be back here for breakfast."

"That's okay then. She ain't too mad. She's just pawing the dust a little bit. How's Rita looking? She still got that dog beauty shop up there in McCook?"

"She looks fine, I guess. I hadn't seen her for so long I almost didn't recognize her. She's got lots of . . . hair. And makeup."

Aunt Louise chuckled. "Well, your mama never was one to hide herself in a brown paper bag. You tell her to come on out here, first chance she gets. I'd like to see her again. She always was good for a laugh. Her and me used to have some good times together when she was living here."

"Well, don't say anything like that to Gramma," I hissed. "She'll bite your face off. I gotta go. Mama's yelling for me."

I hung up, grabbed a can of pop out of the fridge, and ran upstairs.

In just that short time Mama had made the room her own. Her clothes, mostly red and peach and purple stuff, were all over the bed and chair. Daddy's shirts and socks and underwear were stacked on the floor, while sheer pink and black things were stuffed into dresser drawers.

Mama grinned at me over an armload of Daddy's pants and shirts that she was taking out of the closet. She was still damp from her bath. Dark red strands of wet hair curled against her shoulders. She was wearing a psychedelic striped caftan robe, like an Arabian sheikh, only more colorful. An unlit cigarette bobbed from the corner of her mouth.

"Take these on downstairs, will you, darlin'?" she said, dumping the clothes in my arms.

"Here," I said, trying to wave the pop can at her. It was just about covered with clothes.

"Oh, you're a love. No beer in the place, huh? Oh well, this is cold and wet, anyhow."

"Mama, I can't put these clothes in Gramma's room. It's still her room. We were talking about putting Daddy in there when he gets home, but we hadn't gotten to it yet. It doesn't seem right for you to just barge in here and start moving rooms around."

She gave me a long, squinty look, then went on hanging her own stuff in the closet. "Where'd Barb the Barbarian take off to?"

"She went over to Ranger and Louise's for the night, but she said she'd be back in time for breakfast. And she wants you gone by that time."

Mama stopped and stared at me long and hard.

"How do you feel about that, Denny? You want me gone before breakfast, too, or do you want me here to help out when your daddy gets home? Here with my poor crippled husband, where I belong?"

I didn't know what to say. On one hand she was right, and on the other hand Gramma B. was right. I knew all my loyalty ought to go to

Gramma B. But then again, I was fascinated by this person who was my blood mother.

Suddenly she grinned at me, so wide she dropped the cold cigarette from her lips. "Don't worry. You'll get used to me," she said in a flippant tone. "Just help me get this stuff organized, and then we'll sit down and have a good old mother-daughter chat, okay?"

What could I say?

5

Once I got over feeling guilty that I was consorting with the enemy, so to speak, I started enjoying Mama. She bossed me around, but in a cheerful way, and she did twice as much work as I did.

While I piled Daddy's clothes in the other bedroom, trying not to look at the bed where Tyler and I had . . . trying not to think about Tyler at all, Mama brought in the rest of her stuff from the hatchback, tied Muffy to the porch rail so she could do her business for the night, found places for the plants on the kitchen windowsill, and finished unpacking her three suitcases.

We ended up sitting at the kitchen table, Mama eating baloney sandwiches and me finishing off the remains of a bowl of tapioca pudding.

"I want you to call me Rita," she announced. "I left you in the care of strangers when you were just a little thing, and I don't deserve the title of Mama." She said it with no remorse, just stating a fact.

"My daddy and Gramma, not hardly strangers," I said, scraping the bowl. Muffy, who was in now, sat up and begged with her eyes fastened to the pudding bowl.

"Go on. Put it down on the floor for her. She'll clean it so good we won't have to wash it."

I gave her a startled look.

"Just kidding, darlin'." She grinned and took the cigarette out of her mouth to wave it gracefully through the air. It still wasn't lit. Gingerly I set the pudding bowl on the floor for Muffy. It was bigger than she was, but she managed.

"How come you don't light that thing . . . Rita." The name sounded funny for me to say, but it did suit her better than Mama.

"I'm kicking the habit. It was making my skin look old. Hell, I'm only in my thirties. I'm not ready for lines and wrinkles yet a while."

"So what about your grooming shop up there in McCook? Have you got somebody to run it for you while you're gone, or what?"

Muffy had the pudding bowl shoved clear across the floor and cornered up against the stove. She had her front feet inside it and was going after the last little bit of flavor. I made a mental note to get it up off the floor and thoroughly scrubbed before Gramma came home.

Rita's face got serious. "I've had to give up my thriving business, darlin'. When I got that call from your daddy, my heart just told me, 'Rita, you know where your duty lies, and you're going to go down there and do it.' I just hung out the Closed sign, canceled my appointments, and came on down here."

"What about where you lived?"

"In back of the shop there? Yes, well, of course I hated to leave my little nest, you know, but what choice did I have? I figured to borrow a truck or stock trailer or some such and go back up there this weekend maybe, clear out the big stuff. My TV and entertainment center and all that. And of course, the shop equipment."

I looked up from watching Muffy's pursuit

of tapioca, which had now led her and the bowl back across the kitchen and into the hall by the bathroom.

"Shop equipment?"

"Sure. What'd you think—I was going to move off and leave that stuff? Listen, I've got a six-hundred-dollar grooming table, hydraulic lift, fingertip swivel action, lighting from underneath. It's the Cadillac of grooming tables. I wouldn't go off and leave that baby. Not to mention about a thousand bucks' worth of clippers and blades and shears. I've got one pair of German cold-steel shears I paid two hundred bucks for. And three dryers, four cages, not to mention a complete selection of earbows and nail polish."

"Yes, but what are you going to do with all that stuff down . . . here . . ." I was beginning to get the drift.

The cigarette was making bird swoops through the air again, in Rita's bony hand. "I figured I'd set up in the back of the saddle shop. It'd be perfect. I'll hang a sign out by the highway, run a few ads in the newspaper, and presto, a booming business with no overhead. I've been paying five hundred bucks a month rent on my shop, up there in McCook. That's thirty-three poodles, right there."

I gave her a long look. "What about taking care of your poor crippled husband? Wasn't that what you were coming back for?"

She jumped up and went into the hall to fetch the pudding bowl, which was on its way into the bathroom with Muffy's front end inside it, her teeth scraping frantically for one last taste of tapioca. Depositing the bowl in the sink, Rita scooped up the dog and sat back down to face my question.

"Of course that's what I came back for," she explained. "To take care of Doe and to see you through this crisis."

I was in a crisis all right, over my crippled daddy, *and* over Tyler Oneota. What was he doing right now over there in Stillwater? And why didn't he love me as much I loved him, the bastard?

"The thing of it is," Rita went on, "with the dog-grooming business, you can schedule your clients any time you want them. I'll have time to help you and your gramma take care of Doe, and times when I'm not helping out there, I can be in the shop making money. Doesn't that sound ideal?"

It had its points. Especially the money part.

"But what about Gramma B.?" I asked. "She wants you out of here by morning, and she wasn't kidding. This is her house after all. What are you going to do about that situation?"

She leaned back in her chair, tilting it dangerously, and put her bare feet up on the chair between us. I did the same; our feet shared the chair. It gave me a closeness feeling. I couldn't imagine hugging this little slivery woman like I hugged big old soft Gramma B., but it was oddly nice being close to her feet. The toenails were painted deep purple.

"Barb will get over her snit," she said confidently. "The house belongs to Doe legally; she knows that and I know that. Your grampa left Doe the house and land when he died, with the clause in the will that Barb could live in it till she died if she chose to.

"That will got your Uncle Ranger's tail in a twist, believe me. Doe and I had just got married when all that came to a head. Doe was the favorite son because he'd gone off rodeoing, like old Bill always wanted to but couldn't. I never knew him very well. He got killed just after I moved in here. But my theory on Bill was that he had these two sides to his nature, see, the wild reckless skirt-chasing rodeoing side where he fantasized about the old west and all that crap. Doe fulfilled that side of his daddy's nature. And then there was the other side, being responsible and taking care of home and family and all that. Ranger was like that. Doe told me that him and Ranger both grew up wanting to rodeo. Told me Ranger was actually better at it than he was, but he didn't have the guts to go after the big dream. Stayed home, rented that little place north of town, and more or less lived out his life the same as old Bill had.

"But Bill never did get over wanting to be that other kind of man, like Doe was. So he favored Doe and left him this place when he died."

I thought about that for a while.

"Did Uncle Ranger really get mad?" It was hard to imagine him mad.

"Oh, for a while there. Hurt more than mad, probably. He'd spent his life trying to please his daddy and never did get to be the favorite. The will just proved that. I don't think he cared a whole lot about the property. And his wife was such a good-natured soul, nothing ever torqued her shorts. She still there?"

I nodded. "I talked to her a while ago, to tell her Gramma was on her way. She said to tell you to come on out for a visit when you get the chance. Said she always liked you. You were good for a laugh."

Rita tilted her head back and cackled.

"So what about you?" she asked, suddenly fastening her little eyes on me. "Tell me all about your life and times. How many boyfriends you got?"

"None at the moment." I looked away.

"Aha. Let me guess. You just broke up with somebody, right? Tell me about him."

"I'd rather not. It just happened lately. I don't feel like talking about it yet."

"Sure you do. You're my daughter, aren't you? Talking's in your nature, girl. What was his name, what'd he look like, who dumped who and why?"

I sighed. She was right. I did want to talk about him. I just wasn't sure her ears were the right receptacles. "Tyler Oneota. Very good-looking."

"In school? Out of school? What's he do?"

I lowered my head and studied the blackened soles of her bare feet. Time to clean the floors, looked like.

"He's Daddy's roping partner. *Was* Daddy's roping partner."

She banged her pop can on the table. "Girl, what are you using for brains, tapioca pudding?

You lived with your daddy all those years, and you didn't learn sense enough to sail clear of rodeo ropers? I bet he was handsome as hell, wasn't he? I bet he fed you such a line. Hell, I was twenty when I met your daddy, but I didn't have no better sense, either, so I guess I shouldn't expect it of you. Well, you're probably smarter than I was, after all. You broke it off with him before he ruint your life, like Doe ruint mine."

I didn't say anything. At that moment I wasn't sure how much of my life *was* ruined. I could be pregnant, and that would be a lifelong consequence, for sure, for sure. A scary one. Or I might be so hung up on Tyler that I never could get him out of my system. Never could love anybody else for the rest of my life. What then?

Or I might be already starting the healing process, and I might be able to go on from here, sadder but wiser.

Only time was going to tell.

Wednesday, July 12

1

Sun B-Q started my day off right by throwing a bucking fit when I tried to force her into a flying lead change. The morning workout had been going fine till we started on the figure-eighting. Then she got humpbacked and lashy-tailed and cranky. I walked and trotted her through a couple of eights, and she seemed to relax, but she tightened up again when we went into the first circle at a slow lope. When we got to the changeover spot, she just plain out rebelled, and before I knew it, I was spitting dust off my mouth and picking myself up from the ground.

"You break anything?" a voice called from the fence.

It was Mama. Rita. It wasn't even six o'clock yet, and there she was in her embroidered jeans and a full makeup job that must have taken half an hour, what with the eyebrow penciling and eyeliner and two shades of purple shadow. And combing through that straw stack of hair must have taken another ten minutes. Who did she think was going to see her?

"Who d'you think is going to see you?" I asked meanly as I hobbled after Sunny. "You might as well save your time and your makeup, Rita. You're in the country now, you know."

"Well, ain't we grouchy in the mornings." Her voice was almost singsong, it was so chipper.

I ignored her and went back to work on Sunny, practicing easy loping circles left and right, but mostly right. It was exactly like making somebody write with their left hand. She was just naturally a left-footed horse, like most of them, and she felt stiff and awkward leading off with her right foot. But before she could prove herself to the buyer from Tulsa and turn herself into a handful of ready cash, she was going to have to get ambidextrous.

"One more time," I told Sunny through gritted teeth, "and this time you're going to do it. Right?"

With all my mental energy I swung her into the loop, pictured a perfect lead change, and tried to transmit that picture to Sunny. At the turnoff point I shifted my weight and legged her over . . . and she almost did it! There was a little stumble in there but not a buck, and not a big body-twist stumble. It was the closest she'd got, so far.

"Yeah," I whooped, and tried it again.

She bucked. Damn. Back to square one. Hope was looking slimmer and slimmer for her to get her act together in time to pull our fat out of the fire.

This whole thing reminded me of all those kids' books I used to read, where the poor family in Kentucky has just one fine old broodmare left from their once-proud bloodline, and she's in foal to a wonderful stallion by some quirk of plot, and her foal just has to win the big race and pay off the mortgage and make the family solvent again.

And then usually there was a romance angle, too, the girl from the poor family being in love with the son of the rich family next door, but the romance couldn't get itself straightened out either till the colt won the big race.

Only it wasn't ever that simple, was it? What we'd get from Sunny, even if she sold well, would possibly cover Daddy's hospital bill if we were lucky. It wasn't going to do anything about getting him out of the wheelchair and back earning a living. And God only knew what his spirits were going to be like.

And probably in those kids' books the heroine didn't have to wonder if she was pregnant and in danger of having a miscarriage if the wonder colt bucked her off.

The heroine would have been too good and pure to have gotten herself into that predicament in the first place.

Rita disappeared from the fence as soon as I got on Sunny again. By the time I went back to the house, she had the whole kitchen sparkling clean and pancake batter ready to pour in a hot skillet.

Whatever else my mama was or wasn't, nobody could accuse her of being lazy. She practically danced around me, setting the table and flipping her cakes.

We were just tucking into our short stacks when Gramma B. drove in, slammed her car door, and pounded into the kitchen. I froze in mid forkful, suddenly guilty at enjoying Rita's company so much and eating her breakfast. Heck, I'd forgotten all about Gramma B.

I jumped up and scrambled around, setting

another place at the table and getting her a cup of coffee.

"Well, ain't this cozy," Gramma said, staring around at the sparkling kitchen and the pancake breakfast. When it was just her and me, we usually made toast and rinsed clean one of the cups in the sink from the night before.

"Got plenty of batter left," I chirped. Hell, I never chirp. What was the matter with me? "I'll make you a pancake, okay, Gramma? How's everything over at Ranger and Lou's?"

"Peachy keen," Gramma said in a heavy, threatening voice. She was glowering at Rita, who smiled back.

I poured a giant pancake over the whole skillet.

Muffy jumped down from Rita's lap, where she'd been getting bites off her fork, one bite for Rita, one for the dog. She came toward Gramma on stiff legs, her hackles up. With a curly dog like a poodle, it was hard to tell when they had their hackles up, but with Muffy, her ugly expression was a dead giveaway.

Gramma left off staring at Rita long enough to bend down and glare at Muffy. My pancake was bubbling, but I ignored it.

"You show them teeth at me one more time," Gramma said in a deadly tone, "and you're going to be eating them teeth for breakfast. *You got me?*"

Muffy growled but backed away and leaped for the safety of Rita's lap, where she showed her teeth one last, fast time.

"No need to threaten little helpless animals," Rita said. "If we're all going to be living together, we'll just have to learn to get along, won't we?"

The pancake started burning. I got it off the fire and abandoned it to the back of the stove. From the look on Gramma's face, I was pretty sure we weren't going to be sitting down to breakfast together.

"I come to a decision," Gramma B. announced, standing tall and looking straight at me.

"Ranger and Lou invited me to come and live with them," she said.

My jaw dropped. "You're going to do that?"

"No. I ain't going to do that. I just wanted you to know they made the offer. Seeing as how I'm being turned out of my own house." That last was said through her teeth and aimed straight at Rita.

Rita was a vision of calmness. Blandly she

said, "That was not my intention when I came here, Barbara. I did not come into this house with any idea of running you out of it."

"Bullshit."

"No, that was not my idea at all. I thought we'd all work together and get along together. Doe is going to take lots of looking after, you know."

They were locked eyeball to eyeball. I was the only one who saw the big chunk of pancake disappearing off Rita's plate and into Muffy's mouth.

Gramma looked at me, standing with my back against the stove, the spatula like a defensive weapon in my hand.

"Denny," Gramma said, "I will not live under the same roof with this person. If she is going to push in here against all rules of good manners and good taste, then I have no other choice. I will come in the mornings and help out, but I will not live here while *she* is here."

Dead silence, except for the smacking sounds of Muffy finishing off the pancake.

I glanced at Rita just in time to see the flash of triumph before she wiped it off her face.

"Where are you going to go?" I asked.

"I got my eye on a possibility or two in town. I'm going in there right this morning and rent me a nice little apartment, where I can have every damn thing just the way I want it."

She was breathing hard, like she might be working up to a heart attack or something. It scared me. I made a move toward her with the spatula still in my hand.

Gramma waved me off. "Don't say a word, Denny. I'm doing what I want to do. You think I've *liked* living all these years with that damned dead buffalo on the floor? You think I liked going off to sleep every night under a pair of steer horns? That wasn't me. That was never *me*, Barbara Baines. That was just Mrs. Bill Browner. That wasn't *me*."

My jaw was doing a lot of dropping that morning. It did it again. I honestly never thought of Gramma B. as anything but Bill Browner's widow. That was all I'd ever known her as. That and my gramma. My mama, really, all the time I was growing up.

Now here she was saying she hadn't always been thrilled with her marriage and saying she was leaving. It was like she was resigning as my parent.

It was Tyler leaving me all over again, only worse this time because Gramma and I truly did love one another. We'd always been able to count on one another.

As if she read my mind, she turned around fast toward me and took me by the shoulders. "Now you listen here, Denny girl. I love you more than I love anybody in this world. You're not to think of this as me leaving you. I'll be a mile or two down the road, is all. And I'll be here helping out whenever I'm needed. But, don't you see, sweetie, I got no real rights in this house. Not now. So it's time to get my own place. Okay?"

I was wet-eyed, but I gave her a good grin and a long, hard hug.

2

I worked the rest of the colts till lunchtime. Gramma still wasn't back, which meant she'd be eating at the Taco Bell. She was always looking for excuses to eat lunch in town when she went in to run errands, and the Taco Bell was her favorite. She'd get excited just thinking about their burritos.

Rita had put her time to good use, it looked like. The whole house was dusted and vacuumed, and she'd rounded up a stack of cardboard boxes and left them in Gramma's room. For packing, obviously. A little pushy. But on the other hand, we did have to get that room ready for Daddy. He could be getting home any day now.

The phone rang while we were eating lunch. It was the guy from Tulsa, calling to say he was going to be coming through Liberal Saturday afternoon, and how was the buckskin filly coming along?

"Fine," I lied. I gave him directions to our place and said any time Saturday afternoon would be fine.

"Fine," he said, and hung up.

Fine, I thought as I slumped into my chair. That gave me three days to get that little horse shaped up. Whoopee.

After lunch Rita went out to the saddle shop to look around. Muffy and I followed.

"How much business you doing in this place these days?" she asked as we walked through the shop. She ran her fingers over the saddles hanging on the wall.

"Oh, some," I said. "Well, we make a profit of, say, ten, fifteen bucks a day average. Some days we'll make a couple hundred if we sell a new saddle or something big like that. But some days we don't sell a thing."

"Uh huh," she murmured. "You know what your trouble is, don't you?"

I looked at her.

"Your trouble is, you got too much saddle stuff in here."

"That's what it is, Rita. It's a saddle shop, remember?"

"Sure, but what you ought to do is clear out some of that junk"—she waved at the saw-horses holding the old used saddles—"and get some racks of western clothes in here. Make it a western shop, not just a saddle shop. Get us a line of snazzy boots, a couple racks of frontier pants and pearl button shirts. You'll draw a whole lot more people that way. Think how many people buy saddles compared to how many people wear western clothes. Right? Right. This place has an ideal location, right on the highway, close to town. Low overhead, lots of atmosphere. We're sitting on a gold mine here, kid."

I thought about it.

Rita went on through the shop to the back room, where we used to do some repair work. There was an old leatherwork sewing machine and a workbench full of awls and punches and scraps of junk leather that no one had touched for years.

On the other wall was a deep, rusted sink. The rest of the room, about twenty feet square, was just mostly junk that had piled up when no one was looking, shipping cartons that saddles came in, piles of suppliers' catalogs, stacks of boxes of unsold leather cleaner and bits.

"Aha," Rita said. "Just like I remembered

it. Plenty of room in here for my grooming shop. Water, over there, even a usable sink for bathing the dogs, if I can get the rust out. I can put a bank of drying and holding cages over against that far wall and set up my table here in the middle under the light. Leave that wall along there for storage of saddle shop merchandise. Western shop, I should say."

She turned to me, her eyes alight. "Hell, darlin', you and I can work this place together and make a mint of money out of it. I'll teach you to groom, and you can help me out when I'm busy, and you can teach me the saddle business. We can go back and forth. And when your daddy is feeling up to it, he can take over in the western shop, working the cash register and talking rodeo with the customers."

It did sound good.

"What about Gramma?"

"She can do whatever she damn pleases. She won't need to help out at all if she don't want to. We won't need her, darlin'. See? It'll be just the three of us, like a regular family. You and me and your daddy, with Gramma coming to visit. From her own place. You heard her this morning. Seemed clear to me that she wants to move out of here and have her own little place in town. It'll be a nice change for her."

I wasn't sure what I felt about all this shifting in my life. It seemed like Rita was just moving in and taking over, changing the shop all around to suit her whims without even waiting for Daddy to get home. That didn't seem right, but on the other hand her ideas were good. And the prospect of money coming in from dog grooming, from selling western wear along with saddlery, that sounded good to me.

So I wiped the sweat off my face with the tail of my T-shirt and went to work, helping Rita load pile after pile of junk onto the wheelbarrow and haul it off to the barn. That's one of the joys of country living; there's always another building to pile stuff in. We left the leather-stitching machine in place because we did use it every once in a while to sew up somebody's reins that were coming unstitched. Also, it was too heavy for us to shift.

I got a couple of breaks in the labor, once when a bunch of young girls came in to stroke the saddles and leaf through the magazines. One of them finally bought a plastic horse figure of Man o' War. Then again a family of vacationers stopped to use the pop machine and wandered in to ask directions. They didn't buy anything, but they were pleasant to pass the time of day with.

As they left, Rita stuck her head around the corner from the back room and said, "Now see there? If we'd had us a nice display of fringed leather vests and a rack of satin embroidered western shirts, you think that family would've walked out of here empty-handed?"

By late afternoon the back room was empty of everything that didn't have to stay. It was swept down and scrubbed up, and the sink was scoured spotless. I sure didn't inherit my energy level from my mama.

Finally we sort of hosed each other off in that clean sink, got ourselves a pair of Dr. Peppers from the machine out front, and collapsed behind the counter. For a while we talked about how the saddles could be hung closer together on the back wall to make floor space for clothes racks.

"But this is Daddy's shop, don't forget," I said. "You're pushing it with the dog grooming, if you ask me. Not that I don't think it's a good idea. I just think you better haul in a little bit and talk some of this over with Daddy before you go making any more changes."

She snorted. "You leave him to me. I can handle that man."

I wanted to say, "Like you handled him when you were living together?" But I didn't. Rita seemed all crust and confidence, but I had a feeling she could get hurt, just like anyone else.

Instead I said, "How did you and Daddy ever meet, anyhow? I never heard."

She smiled and laid her head way back against the cash register. She had the desk chair; I had the saddle. Her sandaled feet with their purple nails were up against my sawhorse.

"I met him at the McCook rodeo the summer I was twenty. I was working for this vet up there, went to work for him right out of high school. I loved working with the animals, but the job paid so poor, I had to live at home with my folks. So I was still a pretty innocent young thing. I had to work six days a week, didn't have much time or energy to be anything but innocent.

"So I guess I was ripe for the plucking, as they say. My girlfriend and me went to the rodeo, more to look over the cowboys than anything else. Got to horsing around back by the stock pens, and these two young handsome guys come along on their horses and said did we want a ride. So of course we got up behind them on their horses. Just the luck of the draw, I got Adobe Browner.

"Found out later, that was his big thrill, taking girls for rides on his horse. Only I didn't know that at the time. I believed every sweet word that man told me. All the way to his motel room."

"You went to bed with him that first night you met him?" That made me feel slightly better about Tyler Oneota. At least I knew him over a year before he got to me.

She nodded, her eyes still closed. "Yes, ma'am, I did. He told me I was the girl he'd been looking for all his life, and like the damn fool I was, I actually believed him. Gave up my job, broke my folks' hearts, and when the rodeo was over, I went on with Doe to the next one. He was kinda surprised when I volunteered as a traveling companion, but he never said no."

"Then what happened?"

"Got knocked up, of course. What else? He did the right thing by me, as far as marrying me. Brought me back here one night on his way to Colorado, dumped me on his mama's doorstep, and off he went.

"He was in Tulsa the night you were born." Her voice got a tinny edge to it. "We tried to get him on the phone, but he was out partying."

"He never even tried to be a faithful husband?" I asked.

"Not so's you could notice it, he didn't. Not until now."

A slow smile spread over her face, a vindictive smile. The tin in her voice had gone steel.

3

Wednesday was a busy night for our telephone. First, I called Sue while Rita was getting supper on the table. I had to pull the curl out of the cord to get into the bathroom with the phone, where I could tell Sue about Rita without being heard.

No sooner did I hang up from Sue than the phone rang again. In fact, it was still in my hand as I was on my way out of the bathroom.

"Denny, it's Gramma. Listen, I'm over here at Ranger and Lou's for the night. I got me an apartment in town. It's all ready to move into, so I'm going to start moving my things tomorrow."

"That fast?" I could hardly believe she was really doing this crazy thing. Gramma B. living somewhere else. The picture just didn't fit in my head. "Where is it?"

"On Fourth and Willow. It's an old house they cut up into apartments. Nothing fancy, but it's clean and cheap, and there's a nice young couple in the upstairs apartment. You heard anything from your daddy yet?"

"No, not yet."

"Well, listen, see if you can find me some big boxes to pack my things in, will you? I think there's some in the basement."

"Rita already got you a whole bunch of them."

Silence. "Can't wait, can she? She just can't wait to get me out of that house."

I sighed. No point in saying anything.

"I'll be over there first thing in the morning to get my things, and, Denny, you be sure and tell her that everything in that kitchen belongs to me. Every pot and pan, every dish and piece of silverware. And I'm taking them."

I groaned and hung up.

While we ate supper, I told Rita what Gramma said.

"Just like the old . . . She's going to take the dishes right off our table, is she? Thinks we won't have a pot to . . . cook in. Well"— she laughed a nasty laugh—"just wait. I've got kitchen stuff of my own. I'll get a friend of mine to haul everything down here, and we'll be eating off better dishes than Barbara Browner's."

"I wish you two would grow up," I said hopelessly.

"Not a chance, darlin'. She wants war, she's gonna get war."

She jumped up from her chair, spilling Muffy onto the floor, and brought the phone to the table, again stretching its cord to the limit. She dialed and winked at me while it was ringing.

"Darlin'. It's me. Yeah, got here fine, no car trouble except that damn air conditioner kept cutting out on us. . . . Oh, fine. She's a whole head taller than me. I didn't hardly recognize her." Rita sent me another wink.

"Listen, hon, you gonna have any time off the next day or two? . . . Yeah, and I need my stuff down here. Yeah, all of it. The old lady got her tail in a twist and moved out, and she's taking all the kitchen stuff with her, pans and dishes and all like that, so Denny and me's going to be eating with our fingers and cooking on sticks over the fire unless you can . . . Oh, God love you. I knew I could count on you. Can you get your brother to help load stuff?

That grooming table weighs over a couple hundred pounds . . . No, now, you ain't going to lift that by yourself. You get Jeff or somebody to help you. . . . Friday? That would be fine, hon. Okay, write this down. Got a pencil? One mile east of Liberal on Fifty-four, on the north side of the road, big old white house with a saddle shop beside it. You'll see the sign."

Her head dropped, so I couldn't see her face. I got up to start washing the dishes that would be going out of my life tomorrow. Rita's voice dropped to a sexy murmur, with words I couldn't quite make out and soft, rich chuckles.

When she finally hung up, I said, "Who was that?"

"Oh, that was just Chuck. He's a friend of mine."

"Friend."

"Yeah."

"Come on, Rita. Don't give me that bull. He's your boyfriend, isn't he?" I turned to stare her down.

She smiled back, unflustered. "Chuck's my good old buddy. He's been wanting to marry me for a long time now. He'd do just about anything for me."

"Obviously," I said nastily. "He's helping you move back in with your husband. What's a boyfriend for, right? What does Chuck think of you moving back here?"

She stretched, yawned, grinned wickedly at me. "He thinks I'm going to get Doe out of my system, so I'll get the divorce and come back to him."

"Were you living together?"

"Oh no. I had my little apartment there behind the shop, all fixed up just the way I wanted it. There wasn't room for more than one person. And I'm not that crazy about Chuck. He comes in handy, and he's a sweetie and all that. But I'm not about to tie myself down to him."

I sat at the table. This was too important a question to ask while washing dishes.

"Tell me something. Why is it you and Daddy never got a divorce? You've been living separately for, what, eleven years now? How come you never cut loose from each other so you could remarry?"

She tapped a cigarette out of the pack in her shirt pocket and put it, unlit, in her lips. "The answer is right there in the question," she said around the cigarette. "I don't reckon either one of us wanted to be all that free."

"What does that mean? Does that mean you and Daddy still love each other, or what?"

She shrugged and held Muffy up to her face so they could rub noses.

"Well? Rita?"

"Who knows? I have no idea what goes on in your daddy's head. Never did, even when we were living together. He was always telling me he loved me, but then he used them words like somebody else would use howdy. Let's just say that whatever he felt for me, it was never enough to put a crimp in his social life."

There was the tinny edge in her voice again. I could tell there were old hurts still festering in her.

I said, "Well, it looks like you haven't been living in the nunnery all these years yourself. Chucky . . ."

She grinned at me. "I never said I did. Nobody ever expected me to. Listen, I was faithful to your daddy all the time we were together, and what I did after that is nobody's business but my own. Sure I had boyfriends. I'm not dead, you know."

"But you never wanted to marry any of them?"

Her grin faded, and she went back to rubbing noses with Muffy, who looked bored by the whole thing. "After Doe Browner, the rest of them was sort of boring. Now, enough of that kind of talk. Let's get these dishes washed so we can start packing them. We'll leave out enough for breakfast in the morning, and we can eat out till my stuff gets here."

The phone rang while we were working.

"Hi, sugar." It was Daddy's voice, sounding just like his regular self.

"Daddy! How are you? When are you getting out? We've been trying to call, but yesterday they said you were in X ray or something."

"They're letting me out of here tomorrow. Hoyt and them said they'd fly me home. Hospital said I could go any time after noon, so we should be getting in at Liberal around three or so. We'll radio ahead and have the girl at the flying service call you. Okay?"

"Yes, sure. Daddy, how are you? The hospital hasn't told us very much, and we never get an answer when we've tried to ring your room."

"Well, they've either had me in X ray or some therapy deal or other, or else knocked out with sleeping pills. I'm okay. Hell, paralyzed from the hips down, but otherwise I'm wonderful."

His voice got hard toward the end and cracked a little.

"Daddy? Guess who's here?"

The phone was snatched from my hand.

"Hi, hon, it's your little missus. No, no problem. I got here yesterday. No, that's okay. Anything for you, you know that . . . Well, she didn't take it too good. You know your mama. No, listen, it's okay. It's worked out fine. She's found herself a nice little apartment in town . . . No, I didn't now. Don't yell at me. It was her idea entirely. She said she was sick and tired of living with a dead buffalo . . . I am not making it up. Denny was right here; she'll swear to it. Your mama wanted to get a place of her own, and she went out and did it. But she'll still help out when we need her, so don't worry. We'll have plenty of hands here looking after you. . . . See you tomorrow."

We worked silently for a while, each of us following her own thoughts. Finally I said, "Rita, just tell me one thing, will you? Why did you come back here?"

"Lots of reasons," she said in an airy tone.

"That's no answer. Come on. I want to know."

"To take care of my husband in his hour of need."

She said it flatly, so flatly I turned and stared at her. But her face was shut.

4

Sue came over, curious to get a look at Rita. I held my breath, not knowing how they were going to hit it off, but for some reason they took a liking to each other. Sue picked up some newspaper sheets and started wrapping breakables, and first thing I knew we were having a high old time.

Sitting on the floor, packing into a carton the wrapped things we handed her, Rita got to telling stories about the dog-grooming business.

"I'll never forget the time this little Bichon Frise came in for a bath and trim. She felt awful fat to me when I picked her up, and I kind of read her owner the riot act for overfeeding the poor little dog. Well, I give her her bath and I've got her on the table, see, roughing her down with the scissors, and all of a sudden this dog starts going into labor. I'm not kidding. She started whining and fighting me, trying to get at her rear end, and before I figured out what her problem was, she'd popped a puppy out, right there on the table. Well, I got her in the drying cage as fast as I could and called up her owner and told her. What do you think she says? She says, 'Cottontail couldn't possibly be in a family way.' I says, 'Look, lady, she's had three puppies already and more on the way. If that's not in the family way I'd like to know what is.' "

Sue and I laughed along with her.

"Well, this woman says, 'But Cottontail wasn't around any boy dogs, except my neighbor's beagle, and she wouldn't have done anything like that with a dog that wasn't her own kind.' "

We were all whooping and waving our arms and bending double, trying to get our breaths. Muffy barked with the joy of it all.

"Well, that's not even the funniest. There was the time a guy tried to hire me as an assassin."

"What?" Sue and I shrieked together.

"My mama the hit man?" I howled. A whole lot of tension was easing out of me with all this laughing. It didn't matter whether the stories were actually all that funny; it just felt so damn good to be laughing with friends on a kitchen floor on a hot summer night.

Sue said, "Don't stop there. Who did you have to ice?"

Rita got her breath back and went on. "This couple come in the shop one day. They're on vacation, see, just your average nice middle-aged couple from Ohio or someplace. Got this red cocker spaniel. Arthur, his name was. They were staying over for a day while they got their car worked on, and they wanted Arthur to have a bath and trim. He had yeast infection in his ears, and a lot of sour food-gunk stuck in the bottom part of his ears, where they'd rub along his mouth and pick up food and saliva and junk. A cocker's ears can get pretty rank if you let them go.

"So anyway, they leave the dog with me, and about half an hour later I get this phone call, from the husband. He says he'll slip me a hundred bucks if Arthur has an accident—you know, hangs himself in the grooming noose or gets fried in the dryer or some such. Accidents like that can happen in a grooming shop. You go off and leave a dog standing on the table with his head in the grooming noose, and he jumps off the table and breaks his neck or hangs himself. I've known it to happen to other groomers, but I never had anything like that happen to me because I know better than to do stupid things like that. That was the first thing they taught us at Shears R Us. That was the grooming school I went to, in Kansas City, after Doe and I split up."

"Never mind that," I said, kicking at her, "what about Arthur? Did you do it?"

She squinted up at me, and suddenly the fun was gone from the room. "Of course I didn't do it. What do you think I am? The guy hated his wife's dog. That's his problem. My guess was the dog slept on the bed with them, and the guy was fed up with it or something. I couldn't kill a dog. I told him where he could put his hundred bucks."

She glanced quickly at me, a funny, questioning glance. We really didn't know each other at all. I couldn't tell if she was hur that I thought she might kill a dog, or what.

Rita started another story just as the phone rang once again.

It was Tyler.

My heart was so high up in my throat, I could hardly get words out past it.

"How y'all doing?" he asked.

"Good. Fine. How's it going over there? Did you do good?" My heart was down out of my throat now, but it was banging so hard I could hardly hear Ty.

"Done real good today, and fairly good yesterday. Me and A.J. never worked together before, and it always takes a while, you know. He's a little quicker out of the chutes than Doe was, and he's got a tendency to overshoot me and have to pull up. We got third yesterday, and today I got Sioux off the mark a little faster than she was used to, and A.J. held back just a hair, and we come out right. Got first money today."

"Terrific," I said. What was he calling for? What about me?

There was a noise behind him, music and shouting voices. He was calling from a bar, obviously.

"Heard anything from your daddy yet?" he asked.

"Yeah, he called tonight. He's coming home tomorrow. Hoyt and them are flying him back."

"How's he sound?"

"Daddy? Sounded pretty normal. Not happy about being paralyzed."

"No. Well, can't blame him for that."

"No."

When was he going to say something about me? I gripped the phone so hard, my knuckles went white. Sue was watching me with knowing eyes. I moved around the corner into the bathroom.

"Babe?" His voice got softer, like he was leaning in closer to his phone as I was with mine.

I held my breath. I needed him to say something to *me*, something about our closeness. I needed to know from him that I wasn't just another roll in the hay that he'd already forgotten about.

"Listen," he said, "would you look in that top dresser drawer and see if I left my razor? I swore I packed that thing, and now I can't find it anywhere. Would you do that for me?"

"Yes," I said in a wooden voice.

"Good. Get a pencil and write this down. I'll be at the Holiday Inn at Lawton this Saturday and Sunday. Send it to me in care of them. Okay? Got that?"

"Yes," I said. But I didn't. I didn't write it down, and I wasn't going to send the damn razor if I did find it in the dresser drawer. He could just go to hell.

"Thanks, babe," he said, and hung up.

Sue and Rita were silently waiting as I came out and hung the phone back up on the wall.

"Ty?" Sue asked.

I nodded.

Rita said. "What'd he want?"

"His razor. And he asked how Daddy was."

"That was all?" Sue said.

"That was all."

We worked a while more, but the fun was gone out of it. When Sue got up to leave, I walked her to her mom's car. We leaned against the side of the car for a while, just looking up at the stars. The sky was still red along the western horizon, but the rest of it was blue-black and full of stars.

"He never said anything personal?" Sue asked finally.

"Nope."

"You know, don't you, that he's not worth the ground you walk on and your job is to forget him now, get him out of your system."

I smiled. "And *you* know that that's the same advice every best friend gives at times like these, and it doesn't mean a damn thing. I don't know that he's not worthy of me. For all I know, I wasn't worthy of him, or I could have hung onto him."

She just shook her head. "Wrongo. Wrongo."

"He's a lot better looking than me. I mean, he's handsomer for a man than I am pretty for a girl. If you know what I mean."

"No he's not. There's nothing wrong with your looks, Den. Take my word for it. I've got great taste. Do you think I'd hook up with somebody dorky? You've got pretty hair, good eyes, perfect skin, damn you, nothing wrong with your figure, except you're bowlegged from all that horseback riding."

I laughed and hit her in the arm. "Get out of here. I'll cure my own broken heart. Thank you very much."

She got in the car, then gave me a long, warm look. "You will, too. Let a little more time go by, and you'll get over that bum. What I figure is, every woman starts out her love life by falling for some wrongie, some handsome no-good drifter. And then when you've healed up from that one, you're ready for true love with the right man."

I grinned. "So what was with Norman?"

She grinned back. "He wasn't wrong enough for my first love. He's the one I should fall in love with later on, after I've broke my heart over somebody like Tyler Oneota."

We looked at each other silently.

"I'll loan him to you," I said.

She hooted and drove off toward town.

5

"Darlin', you're running east looking for a sunset."

"Huh?" I said.

It was bedtime, and I was all showered and wet-haired, but too restless to get prone. Tyler Oneota had wakened a hunger in my body that hadn't been a problem before, but it was now. I didn't want to get prone alone. That was the bottom line.

So after Sue drove off, I hosed down in the shower, pulled on my nightshirt, and came back downstairs and out onto the porch. The TV was on in the living room, Johnny Carson doing one-liners, so I figured that's where Rita was. I wanted to avoid her for a while, just to rest up from all her energy.

But she was sitting on the edge of the porch, back against the house, one leg dangling in the marigolds and swinging. She had a dead marigold head between her toes. The unlit cigarette showed up white in the starlight.

We sat without talking for maybe five minutes before she popped out with that line, for no reason.

"Darlin', you're running east looking for a sunset."

I said huh and turned to squint at her through the dark. "What's that supposed to mean?"

"Means," she said patiently, "that what you want is against all the laws of nature, and it ain't never going to happen, no way, no how, so you might as well quit running east and thinking you're ever going to get you a sunset thataway."

"Okay, now do you want to translate that? I've got no idea what you're talking about. All I was doing was sitting here not saying a word."

I moved around on the splintery wooden porch chair, pulling the tail of my shirt down a little farther. It was my favorite and only nightshirt, with a picture of a horse lying in bed with the covers over him and his four little horseshoes on the floor beside him, nails up. But it wasn't really long enough to protect me from chair splinters unless I was careful. I remembered Ty's hands smoothing down my bare legs . . .

"I'm talking about that cowboy of yours," Rita said, cutting into my thoughts like a rusty knife. "You've had the fidgets all night, ever since he called, so it's obvious to me that you haven't even begun getting over him. Now according to my theories, that means you're still holding out some hope of getting him back. Am I right?"

"No," I said dully. "I know what kind of guy he is."

She sat forward and looked at me intensely, holding her cigarette in her long, thin fingers and waving it for punctuation.

"Now there you're lying to yourself. Some little part of your mind still isn't facing facts, and you're not going to start getting over this ole boy till you understand him. So just listen to me because I am a past master at guys like him.

"So far you've been looking at this love affair, or whatever you want to call it, just from your own set of eyes. Am I right? Any girl your age that hasn't been in love yet has got a whole load of romantic daydreams she's been building up in her head. You read romance books, right? Watch a few soaps on the tube? Somewhere along the line you've been infected with this notion that the love of a good woman is going to change that handsome rascal into a devoted, faithful lover."

She was hitting the nail right on the old thumb so far. I listened in spite of myself.

"Okay now, darlin', just try to take the blinders off for a minute and put yourself in Tyrone's place."

"Tyler."

"Whatever. Just close your eyes and imagine you were him. Okay now, here goes. You know you're a hunk. You look at yourself every morning in the mirror when you shave, right?"

I grinned but kept my eyes shut.

"And you've been a professional rodeo roper for, what, three or four years, something like that. So right there you've got a guarantee of getting just about any girl you want. You're handsome as hell, and you're in a glamour profession where the public, including the sexually active young female public, comes to watch you perform. Not unlike a rock star, right?"

"Spot on, inspector," I said in my British accent.

"So anything you can get all you want of, anytime you want it, you're not going to put much value on it, are you? It's offered, you take it, but you really don't think much about it. It's kinda like eating your meals. You take it for granted that the next meal is going to appear as soon as you're hungry, and you don't really need to fall in love with your mashed potatoes the same way a starving person would."

I quit smiling. "You're saying I'm mashed potatoes?"

"No, I'm saying that when you look at it from his viewpoint, you should be able to see that what you thought you were giving him, and what he thought he was getting, were two different things. Both equally understandable! See? It's natural that you thought it was a big deal, love and romance and your virginity . . . I'm guessing on that."

I nodded, sighing.

"Okay, love and romance and your virginity was what you were giving. That's natural. But just another lunch was what he was getting, from his point of view. Maybe someday he will fall in love and settle down, but for now he's got everything he wants, with no strings or responsibilities, and plenty of variety to make a spicy life. So it's just a fact of nature that he's not going to put the same value on whatever you two had going as you put on it. Fact of nature, which I'm just now learning for myself in my old age. Sunsets are in the west. You only do yourself harm knocking up against it."

We sat without talking for a very long time, maybe a record for Rita. Muffy came over to sniff my leg, so I picked her up and held her. She nestled down on my stomach and made me feel a little better, just being warm and friendly. I could almost see why Rita was so attached to her.

Rita went on in an offhand voice, talking up at the stars more than at me. "You know, years ago people got married and stayed married till death did them part, and you want to know why? My guess is it was because they didn't have as many choices as we've got. They'd grow up on farms or in little towns, maybe never travel more than twenty miles their whole lives, and not know more than a hundred people. They'd pick out a husband or wife from among maybe three or four possibilities and settle down with them and make do for the rest of their lives.

"And they needed one another for the daily work of survival. A woman had to have a man's protection because there weren't jobs for her, and a man needed a housekeeper because the work was a full-time job, all that bread baking and floor scrubbing. An unmarried man couldn't drive down to the laundromat with a week's wash or pick up a bunch of frozen microwave dinners."

"So what's your point?" I asked in the same detached voice. I was more than half thinking about Tyler and what she'd said about his outlook.

"My point. My point is that we females tend to hang onto that old-fashioned notion of permanent love because it fits in with our nature as nest builders and family raisers. So we keep getting hurt. We need to modernize our expectations."

I didn't want to. I wanted true love forever after, and a big part of me still wanted it to be Tyler. And yet, I knew that everything Rita was saying made sense. If I was in Ty's position, with somebody new falling in love with me every town I hit, every week, wouldn't I get an awful ego charge out of it? Wouldn't it be a high, looking down from my horse at all those adoring groupies? Wouldn't I enjoy it to the hilt while I was young?

Damn straight I would.

There was a kernel of comfort in the thought.

I began to feel a little less like a failure.

Thursday, July 13

1

Sun B-Q started the day off well. She worked pleasantly for me and even did her figure-eights and changed leads, but she'd drop back to a trot for a step or two, going cautiously onto the new direction. She wasn't stumbling or bucking, but she wasn't taking those flying changes that a good cutting horse would do as easy as breathing.

If you've got a calf cut out of a herd, and you have to dodge back and forth and make lightning dashes and spins to keep that calf from getting back to his herd, and if you're doing it in the show ring with prize money and glory in the balance, you don't take the time to slow to a trot whenever you need to switch gears. Fact of life. Like the sun always sets in the west.

But at least she wasn't fighting me today. That was some progress; her acceptance of the routine.

I left the other colts unworked and spent the rest of the morning with Rita and Gramma B., packing cartons and hauling them into town to the new apartment.

They were hurrying to get the bedroom cleaned out before it was time to go pick up Daddy at the airport. They seemed to be getting along tolerably well, maybe because Gramma was off to town with another load of stuff every hour or so.

When Rita came across the boxes of Starlite Lingerie, she dropped what she was doing and said, "What in hell is this stuff? Denny? What'd you do, buy out Frederick's of Hollywood for that cowboy of yours?"

"It's not my stuff; it's Gramma's," I said, coming through the dining room with an armload of clothes from the closet. On Gramma's whispered orders I was taking the hangers, too.

Rita's jaw dropped. "Get out of here."

"No, it really is Gramma's stuff. She sells it. She has people host parties for her, lingerie parties, you know, like Tupperware or Mary Kay cosmetics. She sells the stuff."

"Get out of here," Rita scoffed again, a huge

grin spreading across her face. "Hah. I knew there was something I liked about that old broad. It's taken me twenty years to figure out what it was . . ."

She spent the next half hour taking out all the samples in the box and holding them up to herself. "Hey, I love this one, don't you? God, Chuck would just die if I wore something like this."

Gramma was off to town with a load just then.

"I'm going to buy this one," Rita said. "Black is my color. I love it. Hoo-eee, I could get any old boy I wanted with ammunition like this."

"Hey, Mother dear, aren't you forgetting something? Like a crippled husband arriving this afternoon for you to take care of and be faithful to?"

Her face closed for an instant; then she laughed and flipped the black lace baby dolls in the air.

"Just because he's half dead don't mean I am," she said. I didn't ask her what that was supposed to mean. I didn't want to know.

When Gramma came back, we fixed the clothes rod across the back of her car and hung all her closet clothes on it. Then we went back into the house, her arm riding on my shoulder in an unusual gesture of affection. All morning I'd been trying to read her mood, but all I could see was blandness. She didn't take verbal potshots at Rita; she just went calmly about the business of stripping our house of everything that she considered hers.

Now, while Rita stirred up sloppy joes for lunch, Gramma and I stood together in the doorway of her former bedroom. It was stripped bare, empty closet, empty dresser drawers, no gowns or robes hanging from the steer horns. No blue rug over the buffalo.

We stood there for the longest time, she in a mood and me not wanting to break it for her.

Suddenly she pulled in a long breath, sighed it out again, and marched into the room. She bent and began rolling up the buffalo hide.

"Give me a hand with this, Denny. It's a hernia-maker."

"You're taking the buffalo?" I asked, astounded. "I thought you hated its guts. Not that it has any guts left, of course."

"Shut up and help me. Lift up on that corner of the bed, there, while I pull this thing . . ." She grunted over the rug, jerking it loose from the dresser's foot, and folding it in on itself. I lifted the bed like a good girl.

"How come you decided to take it?" I asked again.

"That apartment don't seem right without this damn stupid ugly thing in it. I don't want to lose your grampa completely, the old bastard. Here, take one end of the roll. I think we can stuff it in the trunk if we tie the lid down over it."

I followed her through the house on the back end of the rug roll. "Are you taking the steer horns, too?" I asked in a voice that was almost timid.

"Yes," she snarled. "Got to have somewhere to hang my night things, don't I? I don't want to hear another word about it."

She got her wish.

After lunch the three of us kept an uneasy truce while we waited for the phone to ring. Gramma watched her soaps; Rita changed the sheets on the bed that would be Daddy's. I moved around the house, looking out windows, trying to read the new *Western Horseman*, but not being able to concentrate.

All three of us were suddenly centered on Daddy. We'd had our own little distractions up till now, but we couldn't put off thinking about Daddy any longer. He was going to be here in another hour or two, and he was going to be damaged beyond repair. How was he taking it? What was his spirit going to be like from now on?

What was his life going to be worth to him if he couldn't ride horses and rope steer heels and take women to bed?

I couldn't even begin to imagine what he was going through.

One thing I did know—what he was facing right now purely dwarfed my heartbreak over Tyler. Daddy's tragedy was real. Mine was just another foolish girl throwing her heart on the bed and getting the dumping she was asking for.

When the phone finally rang, it scared us all out of our skins. I got to it first.

"Denny? This is Jan, over at the flying service. Listen, Hoyt and them just called in. They're about a half hour out."

"Okay. We're on our way. Thanks, Jan."

We three started for the door and collided in the doorway. Gramma was wearing her usual baggy elastic-topped jeans and her husband's shirt, but Rita had changed into a very short purple skirt and one of those tops that doesn't come all the way to the waist, so there were flashes of bare Rita showing around the middle.

"We'll take my car," Gramma said. "It's bigger."

"Wait a minute," I said. "If Hoyt and them are coming back here, we're going to need both cars. Three of them plus Daddy and the wheelchair, plus us three."

"I'll follow you in mine," Rita said. "Hell, I know my way to the airport. I'll just meet you there. You riding with me, darlin'?"

I hesitated on the bottom step. Loyalties! But this had to be Gramma's day. I was about to lose her, at least the all-day everyday part of having her in my life. I rode with her.

We made it through town in record time and pulled up beside the flying service building, off a ways from the terminal, where the little commuter airlines ran flights to Tulsa and Kansas City and Denver.

Jan, the girl behind the counter, waved at us, but we didn't have time to go inside and say hi. Already Hoyt's little Comanche was coming down out of the sky, taxiing toward us . . . bringing Daddy home.

2

"Hoyt and them" was a pretty loose term that had come to mean Hoyt Ramirez and whoever was currently traveling with him. Hoyt owned the Comanche, and whoever was riding with him would pitch in on the flying expenses. They were all professional riders, either saddle bronc, bareback bronc, or bulls, so they traveled light. Their saddles and riggings and a bag for their clothes was all they needed. They could pile three or four guys and their gear in that Comanche and hit twice as many rodeos as the ropers and bulldoggers, who had to drive and haul their own horses.

Hoyt and them would stop off at our place maybe half a dozen times during the season. They'd spend a day doing their laundry, making phone calls, which they always paid for, and messing around with our horses and calves. Hoyt would spend a few hours with the mechanics at the airport, tinkering with the Comanche, which was getting considerable age on it by now, and the next day they'd all be off again. They were good guys, whoever the "them" part of the team happened to be.

We three women stood around as close to the plane as we could safely get while they chocked the wheels and started opening doors. Hoyt jumped down first and came sprinting around the fuselage to hug Gramma and me and to do a quick sort of hat-tipping half bow toward Rita. He was an older guy like Daddy, probably in his middle forties, but dark and lean and hard as could be. Handsome, whew, he'd take your breath away if you looked at him in that light.

"I'm sorry about Doe's accident," he said in his soft, quick voice, aimed mostly at Gramma B.

Then he spun and started helping the other two men get Daddy out of the plane's door and into a folding canvas wheelchair that came out of the luggage compartment. There, finally, was Daddy being lifted down and set into the chair.

He looked just like himself. I was surprised.

I don't know what I expected, wounds or bandages or something. Hospital pallor at least. But he was his usual sun-browned self, only in a sitting position instead of standing.

We all went forward one at a time to give him a hug and kiss, his mother, his wife, his daughter. I'd have thought we'd all be bawling, but none of us was. His strong arms reached up and hugged me as we kissed each other on the cheeks.

All I could think of to say was, "Hi, Daddy."

When I pulled away to where I could look at his face, I could see his eyes were wet.

We all sorted ourselves out then and headed for the cars. The other two guys had both been at our place before, Jimmy Dean Turnquist and Polk something-or-other. Jimmy Dean was a lot of fun, always kidding around and telling awful jokes. He was real tall, with sandy hair and a growing bald spot. Polk was quite a bit younger and so shy I hardly remember him ever saying a word. He was smaller and redheaded and had pretty bad acne scars on his face. But he was one of the top bull riders in the country, and that's as dangerous as it gets, so there was obviously more to him than met the eye.

Hoyt went into the office to talk to the flying service guys, while Jimmy Dean and Polk got

Daddy loaded into the back of Gramma's car. Jimmy Dean showed me how the wheelchair folded down for traveling. It was neat and easy and lightweight; we had no trouble putting it in the trunk. Then Polk and Jimmy Dean went off in Rita's car while Gramma and I and Daddy and Hoyt followed.

We couldn't find anything to say all the way home. Usually Daddy would be full of talk when he got home, but this time I could hardly ask him how his trip was. That would be like, "But other than that, Napoleon, how were things at Waterloo?"

Going through town, Gramma detoured past Fourth and Willow to show Daddy where her apartment was. We just drove by while she pointed out the house, then circled back onto the highway again.

"No need for you to move out," Daddy muttered. It was just about the first thing he'd said.

"I wanted to," Gramma said in a breezy voice. "About time I had a place of my own. Two women under the same roof is asking for trouble, Doe. You know that. Enough trouble finds us without having to go asking for it."

Nobody said anything.

When we got home, I thought Daddy might want to stay outside awhile, maybe wheel over to the corrals to look at the stock, or at least sit on the porch. After a week in a hospital, that's what you'd expect of an outdoor guy like Daddy. But no, he said he was tired, and he just wanted to lie down and sleep for a while.

I went out to the shop and turned the Closed sign on the door around to Open and unlocked it, checked the water tanks in the pastures, and took a quick look at the horses to be sure everybody was okay. Everybody was.

Hoyt came looking for me and caught up with me in the barn.

"Denny, how you taking all this?" he asked, concern in his eyes. I'd been taking it okay till then, but under his sympathetic stare I felt myself starting to puddle up.

"I'm fine, Hoyt. Thanks for asking. Question is, how is Daddy taking it? He seems so . . . normal, but I know he can't be."

"No, he can't, for a fact. But the docs in Durango have it all set up for him with the hospital here in Liberal, for therapy and outpatient care, and also for counseling sessions. Your daddy's a strong man, honey. He'll make the adjustment. But you know it's going to be hard on you and your family, too. Don't kid yourself about that. Doe's going to have to be helped to the toilet and bathed, and the therapists will probably give him exercises to do, probably some massage treatments that you or somebody will have to do every day. Stuff like that."

I leaned against the barn door frame and stuffed my fingertips into my jeans pockets, and stared toward the house.

From behind me, looking in the same direction, Hoyt said, "I was surprised to see Rita back here. I didn't know they'd patched the blanket."

I shrugged. "I don't know if they did or not. Daddy called her after the accident, and I guess he either asked her to come back or she decided to on her own. She says she wants to take care of her poor crippled husband, but . . ."

Hoyt snorted softly under his breath. After a while he said, "Don't take me wrong, Denny, but somehow I don't see your mama in the role of Sue Barton, Girl Nurse. I'd guess the bright lights and hot music were more to her nature."

"Um. She says she gave up her business in McCook, and her place there and everything, just to come back here and help out. But out of the other side of her mouth she's calling her old boyfriend to help her move her stuff, and she's buying Starlite Lingerie from Gramma. So I don't know what to think."

Hoyt whooped with laughter. "Sorry, honey, I don't mean to make light of your troubles. It was just . . ."

"I know." I smiled a crooked smile. "This is a weird family. Sometimes I don't know what I'm doing in it."

His arm landed gently around my shoulders, and he pulled me against him in a comfortable, leaning-together stance.

"I'll tell you what you're doing in it—you're holding it together is what."

"Nah . . ."

"You are, whether you know it or not. Many's the time your daddy would be on the edge of real trouble, an out-and-out bar fight or a tangle with a jealous husband with a knife in his boot, something like that, and he'd back away from it and kinda settle down again, and I'd hear him mutter something about being Denny's daddy. Couldn't do this to you. That kind of stuff."

"Really?" I loved hearing that.

"And you hold the place together here. I know and you know, and Doe knows, he wouldn't be able to run the horse breeding and training operation without you. Many's the time he's talked about what was he going to do when you left home or got married. Your gramma is fine for running the house, but she couldn't do the horse work, and she don't know enough about the saddlery business to order stock and run the shop.

"And beyond that, if you ask me, you are one member of this family that's got her feet planted firm on the ground. You've got good sense, girl. That's a rare and wonderful commodity."

Good sense. Yes. That was certainly me all right. Hopped right into Tyler Oneota's bed, I was so sensible.

Time to change the subject.

"Hoyt?"

"What, hon?"

"Were you there when the accident happened?"

He was silent.

"You were, weren't you?"

"Sort of. There was a bunch of us."

"What happened?"

Again he was silent.

"Come on, Hoyt. All Daddy said was that he had a fall at the rodeo. But some guy in the shop yesterday said he'd heard Daddy was climbing on the bucking chutes in the middle of the night. Something about women's underwear."

I could feel Hoyt's body deflating against my side as the air went out of him.

"Well then, I guess if you've already heard that part . . . It was just stupid horsing around. We'd been out partying a little, you know. Your daddy'd had his snoot in the pop, and he was feeling pretty good. We ended up back at the rodeo grounds, and Doe got it in his head he wanted to hang a brassiere from the hands of the time clock. Thought it would jolly things up, next day."

"Uh huh," I said.

"So there was a lady with us who'd had her snoot in the pop, too, and she obliged with the donation of the garment in question. Jimmy Dean was fixing to do the climbing, but your daddy decided he wanted the honor and the glory. A couple of us tried to stop him. He wasn't in no shape to climb up on that time clock. It was a good twenty feet higher than the chutes. But I guess we wasn't in much better shape, and he got away from us and started up.

"There was a ladder that led up from the catwalk to the clock, and your daddy was halfway up the ladder when he lost it and fell. Landed across the top of a chute, and that was it."

3

It's hard to look at your parent and see him the same way other people do. If you've looked at that one face since before you can remember, it's too familiar to see it clearly.

Adobe Browner was a nice-looking man, though. Even I could tell that. Not handsome, but in some way even more appealing than a handsome man. His nose was a little too big, his mouth too broad and mobile, his eyebrows shaggy. It was a lovable face. Gramma always said he had a Will Rogers quality. You more than half expected him to dig his toe in the dirt and say, "Aw shucks, ma'am, 'twarn't nothing."

But tonight his face looked different. The lines were set deeper. There was almost a gray cast underneath the sun-brown. No, the real difference, I realized suddenly, the real difference was that I'd never seen this face without a smile or at least an animation that was almost a continual smile.

Now all the deep grooves of his face were immobile. His eyes were open and following me, but there was no life in his face. More than anything, I wanted to get out of that bedroom.

But I felt bound to stay with him. Rita, Jimmy Dean, and Polk had gone off to town, no doubt to the Roundup Bar and Grill. Hoyt was on the phone talking to his wife in Bartlesville, Oklahoma. They'd generally talk half an hour or so. Gramma was manning the washer and dryer, keeping track of which load was Polk's and which was Jimmy Dean's. She was an old hand at that.

Daddy had slept through regular suppertime, but woke up hungry about nine, so I'd fixed him up with a rewarmed barbecue sandwich on a paper plate and a beer and brought it on the bed tray we hadn't used since I had the chicken pox in third grade.

I watched him eat in silence. When he was finished, I set the tray on the floor and settled on a corner of the bed. I'd been sitting on the hard straight chair beside the dresser, but the bed looked more comfortable. It had a high footboard to lean against. I'd spent hours of my childhood sitting on that bed with Gramma, talking.

"Does this bother you if I sit here?" I asked him.

He shook his head.

"Are you in pain, Daddy? You have to tell us what you want us to do, okay? We don't know . . ."

"I'm all right," he said. "I don't have any pain. I wish to God I did. My legs are just dead. The rest of me is okay, but I get awful tired."

"Do you want me to go away so you can rest?"

"No, stay. Tell me about the horses. How's the buckskin filly coming along?"

"Pretty good, except she still isn't doing her lead changes, and we're running out of time. Once or twice she's almost had it, you know? I can almost feel her *thinking* it, like her brain is starting to understand what to do, but she just can't quite get the message to her feet. Remember that time I tried to take ballet lessons with Sue when we were little? That was

163

how I felt. I can still remember that feeling, understanding how the teacher wanted me to point my toe but having my foot go off some other way, on its own. I know Sunny'll get it, one of these days. I just don't know if it's going to be in time."

I talked on and on, about Sunny and the others I was schooling, bringing him up to date. After a few minutes he quit listening, but I kept talking anyhow, not quite knowing how to stop.

"Daddy?" I said finally.

"What, sugar?"

"How are we going to make out for money, do you think? What about the hospital bill? Did your insurance cover it?"

He gave a mirthless laugh. "All I've got is Major Medical. In my line of work regular insurance would be so expensive, I couldn't afford it. Rodeo riders are awful expensive to insure, even through the PRCA group plan. All I could afford was the Major Medical, which means I have to pay the first three thousand dollars of any hospital costs. Insurance pays the rest, but I pay the three thousand deductible. And this business ran way over that."

"So you had to pay three thousand to the Durango hospital?" It sounded like a huge amount for just a week.

"I paid what I had, which was the twelve hundred I'd just won in prize money. They agreed to bill me for the rest. I got a guy buying my horse and equipment, but he didn't have more than a few hundred to pay down on him. He's good for the rest of it, but it's going to take some time."

"The guy coming from Tulsa to look at Sun B-Q Saturday, I told him thirty-five hundred for her, like you said. Even if he won't go the whole price, she should bring enough to get clear of the hospital bill."

His sad eyes met mine. "After that we'll just have to do the best we can. The PRCA has a compensation fund for injured members, but I didn't quite get injured during a performance, like the rules say, so I won't qualify."

I grinned then. "It was kind of a performance, Daddy."

It took a while, but his old smile finally broke through. "I see Hoyt's been spilling his guts."

"Listen, the story is all over town. Some guy was in the saddle shop yesterday talking about it. And Rita and Polk and Jimmy Dean are down in town now, probably not keeping secrets very hard."

A shadow passed across his face at the mention of Rita.

Quickly I said, "She's really anxious to help out, Daddy. She wants to set up her dog-grooming business in the back room of the shop, so she can bring in some money while she's taking care of you."

He said nothing.

"And I could skip my senior year if you need me to. Rita was thinking we might add a line of western clothes in the shop, try to turn it into more of a moneymaker."

I watched to see if he was going to get his tail in a twist over the idea of Rita coming in and making changes that way. But he didn't say anything, just looked like he was pondering the ideas.

Finally he said, "I'm not having you drop out of school, girl. You've got some extra credits, though, don't you? I bet if we talked to the school, they'd let you go half days. Wouldn't they?"

I thought about it. We had four morning classes and only two afternoon ones, and if I dropped the extra stuff like music and home ec and phys ed and study halls and just took the classes I'd need to graduate, they would probably go along with that. If I spent my afternoons, say, minding the saddle shop, I could do homework at the same time.

Or Daddy could run the saddle shop. Wheelchair wouldn't keep him from doing that. He'd have the business end of it to keep him busy, the stock ordering and all that. And Rita seemed to think she'd build up a full-time business with the dog grooming. If I was going to school only half days, I could still train the horses and take over that part of the family business. And with Gramma helping out with the housework like she always had . . .

We'd make out.

It was such a load off my chest, I felt downright good.

Then Daddy said, "What about Ty?"

I looked everywhere except at him.

"Ty?"

"Yeah, Ty. Have you heard how he's doing with his new partner?"

"Fine. He called last night and said they got third-place money one day and first the next day. Said the new guy was breaking faster than you did. They had to get that worked out. But he sounded as if he was going to like working with A.J. He asked about you, said to tell you hi."

Daddy looked at me for too long a time.

"What went on between you two while he was staying here?" He asked it in an even voice, like it wasn't an important question.

"Nothing," I lied.

"Denny."

"Well."

"Did that sorry pup mess around with you?"

"No. Not really."

"Well, he better never. He's no good for a kid like you. You want to aim higher than some old rodeo roper."

I looked at him and let a little love shine in my eyes.

"You're not such a bad guy."

"Not for a daddy maybe, but you wouldn't want my type for a husband."

"I know that."

"Look at poor Rita, what I done to that girl. You wouldn't want to end up like her, would you?"

I thought about that for a good long time, then I grinned at him. "If you ask me, Rita is living her life just the way she wants it."

His face darkened. "Yes, I noticed how long

she stayed at my bedside tending to my needs before she romped off to town with the boys."

He heard Hoyt hanging up the phone then and yelled for Hoyt to help him into the bathroom.

I wandered out to the kitchen to help Gramma sort and fold the boys' clothes. I could see why Rita took Jimmy Dean up on his invitation to go to town. I'd have liked to be off myself about now, with Sue and maybe a couple of our friends.

Daddy being cheerful was almost worse than Daddy being grim. It was so sad. I wanted to cry for him, and for myself, too, although that was more of a general grief than a specific one. Tyler had a lot to do with it, but he wasn't all of it.

Life. That was all of it.

As I joined Gramma in her search for matching socks, I said, "Gramma, do you think it's fate, or God, or something bigger than all of us that makes things happen? Do you think Daddy was hurt because he'd been a rounder all his life and it was time for some justice? Or what? What do you believe?"

She snorted and sniffed. "I believe Doe is crippled because he drank too much and tried to pull a damn fool stunt that was bound to get him hurt. We make our own fates, girl, and don't you ever forget it. He's my own son and I love him dearly, and I wouldn't have had this happen to him for anything. But facts are facts. He brought it on himself by being the kind of man he is. Plain and simple. Fate nor God had nothing to do with it."

She was right. I knew it.

Friday, July 14

1

Friday morning was full of comings and goings. I was out at dawn, as usual, working Sunny. She was coming smoother now on her figure-eights, acting like she finally understood what was expected of her, but still breaking her stride for one little step before picking up the new lead.

Rita was up and bright-eyed when I got in the house, already fixing a bacon and eggs breakfast for everybody. Hoyt and Jimmy Dean helped Daddy with his bathroom stuff and dressing, and we all crowded around the table to eat, with Daddy wheeling himself up to the corner of the table. His spirits seemed more or less normal, which was a relief to everybody.

He did run over Muffy's tail, though. Rita had to turn the bacon-watching over to me while she soothed and babied the dog for five minutes.

Gramma B. drove in about eight and took Hoyt and them to the airport since Rita's car was too small. The guys left with smiles and hugs for me, sweet, self-conscious handshakes for Daddy, and fanny pats for Rita. Their stomachs were full, their laundry clean, their socks neatly rolled in pairs. They were happy men.

Daddy wheeled himself out onto the porch, and from there he directed Rita and me through a project of major importance, one that I should have thought of myself. Out of an old barn door and a stout two-by-six left over from some other project, we built a ramp for the wheelchair beside the porch steps.

Rita was surprisingly good with a power saw and hammer. Between the two of us, with Daddy supervising, we had that sucker in place and anchored securely in jig time. I held my breath the first time Daddy coasted down the ramp, but that barn door was solid, and it wasn't too steep a grade for him to get back up it again.

While we had the tools out, we rigged up a little ramp for the one step up from the ground to the low wooden porch of the saddle shop.

Then a two-by-four wedged under the sill was all that was needed for the shop door.

The rest of the morning Daddy and I spent in the shop. I shifted sawhorses and displays until Daddy's chair could maneuver behind the cash register counter or anyplace else he wanted to go. After some chin rubbing and pondering, he decided to give Rita's idea a try and went to work on the phone, talking to people he knew in the wholesaling end of the business.

Just before noon a truck pulled in, and a big, beefy-looking guy climbed down. Rita was all over him like wallpaper, so I figured this must be Chuck, delivering the goods. It was, Chuck and his brother, who apparently had a small trucking business of some kind since the truck had their name on it.

I left Daddy to mind the shop and went to lend a hand with the unloading. There was all of Rita's vivid wardrobe, boxes of hair dryers and nail dryers and electric styling combs and what-all. There were a few chairs and a sofa bed, three small television sets, and boxes of kitchen things.

Last to be unloaded was the grooming shop equipment, the state-of-the-art hydraulic table, a floor-model dog dryer, several cages and crates.

While the rest of them unloaded that stuff, I got to work in the kitchen, unpacking Rita's pans and dishes, starting lunch, and repacking the last of Gramma's stuff in the same boxes.

The only people who talked through lunch were Chuck and Rita. She was leading him in a dance all right, flirting and gushing over him for bringing her stuff down. It was plain as the nose on your face that he was crazy about her . . . and that she was using him in some way against Daddy. Daddy kept his eyes down on his plate and didn't say a word, acted like his mind was somewhere else. But it wasn't. Chuck's brother didn't get into the conversation either, and I didn't even try. I was embarrassed and a little bit ticked off at Rita acting that way, especially right there in front of her husband.

When Chuck went to get into his truck to leave, she gave him such a kiss as I'd seen only on Sue's cable TV Playboy channel.

Daddy wheeled himself right past the show and across the yard and into the saddle shop.

It was a blistering hot afternoon, and what I really wanted to do was stay in the house and read and doze, but there were all those horses out in the pasture just waiting to forget everything I'd taught them if I left them unridden one more day.

I dragged myself through routines with the four of them that needed work the most, a pair of two-year-old green-broke geldings, a four-year-old mare that had a bad rearing habit I was trying to get her past, and a smooth-mouthed mare we'd been using for brood, but who had failed to settle two years in a row. I figured she was pretty enough to make a good kids' show horse, for pleasure classes or equitation, with a little more polish on her gaits.

By three-thirty I was completely out of go. Sweat plastered my clothes to my back and my hair to my face. It stung in my eyes and salted my lips. I wiped the green, grassy spit off the bridle bit I'd been using, hung up the bridle in the barn, and set the incredibly heavy saddle on its sawhorse just inside the barn door. The saddle pad I hung over the fence, inside out, to dry the horse sweat.

Whew.

I pulled out my shirttail and lifted it away from my skin, hoping for a breeze. No such luck. I pulled up the handle on the water pump at the side of the barn and splashed that cold well water over my arms and face and just let them air-dry.

There were cars parked by the shop, three of them. That was a crowd, for us. I went over there and found that business was almost booming. Daddy was ringing up a saddle sale, a used youth-sized single-rigger that we'd taken in on trade for ten dollars and cleaned up and restitched. He was selling it for seventy-five. Yeah for us. A profit today!

Besides the family group buying that saddle, there were two kids I knew from school looking at the leather chaps we had hanging in the corner. I went over to them and told them we were putting in a line of western clothes. They put in requests for their favorite brands of jeans and boots and whispered, "Sorry about your dad's accident."

I could hear Rita talking to someone in the back room, so I stuck my head around the corner.

It was transformed. Even I, who had helped with the clean-out, was surprised at what a professional-looking grooming shop the old back room had turned into. There was the bank of cages against the back wall and the magnificent chrome and glass grooming table, with the fluorescent lights under it, to illuminate the dogs' bellies. There was a rack of scissors and combs and slicker brushes, and three electric clippers hanging from a reel contraption overhead.

And there on the table was an actual dog, with its owner standing out of the way, visiting with Rita as she worked.

The dog was a Bichon Frise, a little white marshmallow of a dog with black button eyes and nose. It had been bathed and blow-dried and was standing patiently with its head in a suspended noose while Rita shaped it with her two-hundred-dollar German cold-steel shears.

She wore a white smock that made her look like a doctor, and she was chatting with the owner as fast as she was trimming the dog.

"This is Barb's neighbor that lives in her apartment building," Rita said to me, by way of introduction.

The grooming table wasn't even bolted to the floor yet, and already Rita had her first customer. The business was going to take off and fly.

Back in the saddle shop, the kids and the family left, and Gordy Watts came in. He was our supplier for the small line of hats, belts, and chaps we'd been carrying. A good-looking guy, Gordy was, and an incurable flirt. He'd been coming on to me since I was twelve, but nobody ever took him seriously.

I went outside and got a can of Dr. Pepper from the machine, using the slugs we kept for that purpose. The sun was far enough west by then to make shade against the building, so I sat there and unwound and half dozed.

The dog customer left. I could hear Rita's voice joining the men's. Daddy had been ordering jeans from Gordy. I'd been half following their discussion of what sizes and how many. When Rita joined them, Gordy's voice got playful, and so did hers. Daddy's voice dropped out of the conversation.

After a while Rita and Gordy came out and strolled to Gordy's car, a station wagon loaded with sample cartons. They didn't notice me. Rita was in full flirting gear, and Gordy was with her every step of the way. They leaned against the car, laughing low and looking into each other's eyes.

I could hear Daddy's chair rolling across the shop, and I knew he was watching, too.

When Gordy finally drove off, Rita sauntered back into the shop, her hips swinging in those white embroidered jeans. She still didn't see me. She was too busy concentrating on herself.

She paused at the door, opened it, and leaned against the frame but didn't go in.

"That's a stud if I ever saw one," she said in a creamy voice.

"Rita, damn you, what are you playing at?" Daddy's voice was harsh.

"I'm just playing your game," she said sweetly. "How does it feel, Doe? How do you like having to sit home here, knowing I can sashay out that door and have any man I want? Knowing I aim to do just that?" Her voice took on the tinny edge. "How do you like knowing I'm free to tomcat around and you aren't, Doe Browner? I had to sit in this house for seven years while you were out skirt-chasing and I was being a mama to your child. Well, now it's my turn to howl, buster."

I was shocked at the anger in her voice.

And I knew, finally, why she had come home.

2

As soon as they were both out of sight in the shop, I got up and went to the house. I pried off boots and jeans and stinky, sweaty shirt, ran my body through the shower, and put on shorts and a clean T-shirt. I left a note on the table saying, "Over the river and through the woods, to Grandmother's apartment I go," then loaded the carton of dishes into Rita's car and took off. Another one of the joys of country living is that people leave the keys in their cars.

Gramma B. was hanging curtains when I got there. The apartment was beginning to look like Gramma's place. At first I hadn't been able to picture her living anywhere but at our house, but now it didn't seem so unbelievable.

This house was not too different from ours

in age and size and personality. Gramma had the whole downstairs, big kitchen, big living room, ugly bathroom, small bedroom. The buffalo went wall to wall in there. I grinned as I looked in the bedroom door and saw that brown hairy floor, the steer horns over the bed. There was a new used bed she'd just bought from the Salvation Army, but it looked just about like her old one at home.

As I held up curtain rod ends for her, I said, "I guess you really loved Grampa, hanging onto his things after all."

"Well, I hated him, too."

"What?"

"Here, hold that up higher. Let me mark where the bracket needs to go. I hated him a good bit, too, Denny. Funny thing was, it never hit me how I felt about him till I went to move out of that house. I'd gone along for years thinking I wanted nothing more than to get away from all those things of his. When time came that I could get away from them, they'd gotten so dear to me, I didn't want to leave them. And I'd never even noticed that my feelings had turned around."

"But why would you hate him? He was a good husband, wasn't he? He stayed home, didn't go rodeoing like he wanted to when he was younger, you told me. He was faithful, wasn't he?"

"Yes and no. Does that answer your question?"

"Gramma," I said, exasperated.

She took over my end of the curtain rod and hammered home the nail that held the bracket. We set the rod in place and stood back to squint for straightness.

"There, that's done." We sat on the kitchen chairs to admire the curtains and their good, straight hanging job. The chairs and table were from the Salvation Army, too.

"Why would you hate him, Gramma?"

She sighed and fiddled with the screwdriver, sliding it back and forth between her fingers. "Oh, maybe hate's too strong a word. I guess I resented him. See, I was riding with him that night when he was killed. We were coming home from the sale barn with a truckload of feeder calves, and he got to going a little too fast down a hill in a freezing rain, missed the curve at the bottom, and rolled the truck in the ditch. We weren't going very fast, you know. It wasn't all that bad a wreck. We both got out of it with just cuts and bruises, but then his heart packed up and quit on him, and he died of a heart attack. The accident had scared him to death, in other words. I guess I resented him for that, for making me be the strong one."

"That doesn't make sense."

"I know it."

We sat silent while I thought about all the adults around me and how they seemed bent on messing up their lives. Was I really smarter than they were or does everybody start out with clear vision and get screwed up later? Then I remembered Tyler and hung my head, mentally, at my own foolishness.

Gramma went on. "You said was he a faithful husband. Well, yes and no. He was a good husband, and he was faithful to me, as far as I know. Never had any other women while we was married. But he wasn't faithful to himself. His nature was to go rodeoing. That was why he always favored Doe over Ranger. He'd set aside that part of himself for my sake and then spent the rest of his life taking it out on me in little ways. He'd put more and more responsibility in my hands, making decisions about money and whatnot, and then resent me for it. I reckon when he died it seemed to me like just one more great big dumping of his responsibilities."

I pondered. "That doesn't make sense. He

couldn't have wanted to die. He probably loved you a lot to give up the rodeo life to stay home and support you."

"Maybe so." She sniffed. "Or maybe he was afraid he would fail at it or get busted up or killed. Maybe I was a convenient excuse. See what I mean?"

"Yeah, I guess."

"Well, that's all water under the dam and over the bridge," she said, standing up. "The main thing is Bill Browner was a good man, and moving over here made me realize how fond I'd gotten of his memory. And that damned buffalo. So. Can you stay and have supper with me?"

I nodded.

"Oh, I forgot to tell you," she went on. "I went grocery shopping this morning and got myself a job as a checker at the A & P. Four days a week, good money and insurance benefits, and I'll get to visit with people. It'll pay for the rent here and still leave me time to have my Starlite parties and give y'all a hand at home."

My Gramma B. was a strong woman. I loved her a whole lot right then.

We had baked beans and cole slaw from the A & P deli, and chocolate mint ice cream.

"How's things out home when you left?" Gramma asked as we scraped up the last of the ice cream.

"I don't know, Gramma. I don't know about Rita. Gordy was there this afternoon, getting the order for the western wear, and she was just flirting up a storm with him. It was indecent."

"And Gordy just hated that, didn't he?"

"You can imagine. But the worst of it was, she was doing it right under Daddy's nose. On purpose. I heard her taunting him with it, Gramma. She was saying stuff like, 'This is what you did to me all those years. How do you like it?' Stuff like that. Rubbing his face in it. I think she means to be as big a rounder as Daddy was, just to get back at him."

Gramma grinned. I wasn't expecting that.

"You know, Denny, I never could warm up to that girl when they were married the first time. I've asked myself why that was, and I think I finally figured out the answer. I was expecting her to change Doe into a domesticated animal, and she failed. Of course it wasn't in his nature, and no woman could have changed that, but I used to have to grit my teeth, watching her all those years just taking it and taking it from Doe and not fighting back.

"When she finally up and left him, I think

I was cheering her on for having the gumption to get out and make her own life. I thought she should have taken you with her, but on the other hand I loved you so much myself, I didn't want to give you up. By that time, though, her and I was in such a habit of sniping at one another, I never could bring myself to say anything nice to her."

It took me a while to absorb all this. I had to open another carton of chocolate mint ice cream, too.

"Are you telling me you're on her side now? You think she's within her rights, tormenting Daddy when he's just newly crippled and has to make that horrible adjustment and all? Are you saying she should be knifing him in the heart like this, just for the sake of revenge?"

Gramma smiled like the wise old woman she probably was. "No. Not really. But keep things in perspective, girl. Your daddy hasn't been in love with her for a long time. Why he called her after his accident I'll never know, but I doubt it was out of love. So I don't reckon she's hurting him any deeper than his pride. The two of them are pretty much cut from the same cloth if you ask me. It just took Rita a few years longer to get her act together. At heart, Rita is a good soul. She cares about people, even if she is a little on the flighty side. Same with Doe. I wouldn't be surprised if they don't settle down after a while, put away the weapons, and fall in love for real. Doe is just a big kid at heart, and Rita is, too. I expect they'll find each other."

After a long quiet time I said, "If they're both such fluffheads, where did I come from?"

Gramma chuckled. "You came from me, girl. Good sense often skips a generation. I've got it, and so have you. You're already well on your way to getting Ty out of your system."

I stared at her while my face turned red.

She slapped me lightly on the arm. "You didn't think you two was getting away with anything, did you? I may be gray-haired, but I'm not deaf, blind, and stupid."

"Oh." I couldn't think of anything else to say.

"Don't worry about it, sweetheart. Like I said, you're already well on your way to forgetting that boy. No, don't argue with me on this. I know you, and I know you ain't really grieving. You didn't truly love him because there wasn't enough there to love, only a good-looking exterior. Hell, we all fall for one or two of those along the way toward growing up.

You've lived through it, and now you're a little older and wiser, and your good sense is going to kick in and take over."

"You think so, huh?" I couldn't stop the slow grin that pulled at my mouth.

Saturday, July 15

It was after two o'clock when the man from Tulsa finally drove in.

It had been a busy morning. Ranger and Lou had been over the night before to see Daddy while I was having supper at Gramma's. By the time I got home, everybody'd gotten over their embarrassment about Daddy's condition and were acting normal. Rita and Lou were talking a mile a minute, and Ranger and Daddy had gone all through the house measuring doorways.

So this morning Ranger showed up with two new doors in the back of his pickup and went to work cutting wider door openings into the bathroom and Daddy's bedroom so he could hang doors wide enough for the wheelchair to fit through easily.

Liberal being a small town, word had already started to spread about Rita's dog-grooming shop, and she'd done a schnauzer and two Shih Tzus before lunch. Fifteen bucks apiece, she told me. And she'd made a couple of saddle-shop sales while she was doing the dogs.

I'd spent the morning on Sunny, clippering off the long hairs on her fetlocks, under her throat, and inside her ears. That was a tussle. She liked the buzz and tickle of the clippers on her nose, though, when I neatened off the whiskers, and she tried to take a taste of the blades. It only made a tiny nick on her lip.

I hosed her down and shampooed her into a lather. She loved that part. I dunked her tail into a sudsy bucket and swished it in circles, spraying water all over the place. I'd taken off my boots and rolled up my pants for the bath job, figuring it was worth the gamble of getting stepped on for the luxury of the wet splashes.

At noon I left Sunny tied in the barn so she couldn't roll and get dirty again. Rita and I threw a pile of sandwiches together, both of us pooped from our morning's work. Then I got into clean riding clothes and went back out to the barn to wait for the Tulsa guy.

With Rita making money hand over fist in her grooming shop and Daddy ordering our new stock of western wear that was going to bring in more money than the saddle shop had ever made before, I felt like I had to sell a horse today or I wouldn't be a full partner in what was shaping up to be a regular family corporation.

As soon as the car pulled in, I knew it was my Tulsa guy. The whole rig just said Tulsa. It was a gray Lincoln Continental, pulling a matching gray-and-silver deluxe horse trailer, and I do mean deluxe.

"You'll be living in tall cotton if you do your stuff right," I murmured to Sun B-Q as we watched from the barn door. I had her in the crosstie ropes just inside the door, where he couldn't miss seeing her.

"Abernathy," he said, by way of introduction. He took my hand and shook it. "You must be the young lady I talked to on the phone. This the filly?"

He went past me and began running his hands over Sunny. He might be rich, but he was a horseman. I could tell that from the way he examined both her eyes, ran his hands down all four legs, and picked up every hoof for a good close look.

"Let's see how she goes for you," he said finally.

I saddled her and jogged into the corral, while he followed, squinting at her rear movement. I loosened Sunny up with a few circles, jogging and loping, with some easy turns and stops. She was feeling good. The bath, the audience, something was tickling her. She tossed her head and collected till her chin was almost on her chest.

Mr. Abernathy called from the fence, "Let's see how she handles her leads."

I put her in a figure-eight, going left first since that was the lead she preferred. Around the circle, back to the switchover point. I reined her right, expecting the break in her stride, but it didn't come! Like a dancer, like a bird on the breeze, she was bending right in a tight circle. A perfect flying lead change! I couldn't believe it.

Back to the center. Another perfect change back to her left lead and on around that loop of the eight. Back in the center, and once again she sailed through a flawless transition, bending the line of her body in mid-stride and leading out with her right foot.

I pulled her down out of it after that. No point in pressing our luck.

I sang inside.

Mr. Abernathy got on her and tried her

out himself, and fifteen minutes later she was loaded in his trailer. I made out the transfer of ownership and ran it into the shop for Daddy to sign.

And there was the check. Three thousand five hundred dollars. It was made out to Browner Ranch, but that was me! I'd done it.

I watched till the Lincoln was out of sight, felt a moment of loss watching Sunny's tail end disappearing, then I kissed the check and took it in to Daddy.

It wasn't till late that night that I realized I'd gone the whole day without once thinking of . . . that guy. What was his name? Tyler something.

I grinned and fell asleep, content.